FOUR OF A KIND

KIND BROTHERS SERIES, BOOK 4

SANDI LYNN

D1528450

SANDI LYNN ROMANCE, LLC

FOUR OF A KIND

New York Times, USA Today & Wall Street Journal
Bestselling Author

Sandi Lynn

Four of a Kind

Photo by Wander Aguiar
Model: Soj M.

❀ Created with Vellum

MISSION STATEMENT

Sandi Lynn Romance

**Providing readers with romance novels that will whisk them away
to another world and from the daily grind of life – one book at a time.**

CHAPTER 1

Simon

"Look at him lying there like a baby," I heard Sam's voice in the distance.

"Yeah. He'd do anything to get attention. He always has." Stefan's voice filtered through the soft beeps of the monitor I was hooked up to.

"Right? He just couldn't stand that all the attention was on my restaurant tonight," Sebastian spoke.

"I can hear you, douchebags," I moaned as I slowly opened my eyes.

"Hey, bro." Sam smiled as he leaned over me. "It's about time you woke up."

Looking to my left, I noticed the sling that kept my shoulder and my arm stabilized, and I felt nothing. Not even a hint a pain except in my back when my body hit the concrete after that motherfucker fired his gun at me. I was still dazed and in a state of confusion.

"The doctor said the surgery went well. He removed the bullet from your shoulder and from what he could tell there isn't any permanent damage," Sebastian said as he sat on the edge of the bed.

"You're lucky, bro, and you scared the shit out of us," Stefan walked over and placed his hand on mine.

"What the hell were you thinking going after that guy without any backup?" Sam asked.

"I was just checking out a tip I received. I didn't see the asshole. His shot came out of nowhere."

"Well, you're lucky he's a shitty shot." A smirk crossed Stefan's lips. "It could have been way worse."

"Mom and Dad were in here for a while. They went to go grab some coffee," Sam said.

"And Roman?"

"Roman was here while you were in surgery. He had to leave, and said he'll be back."

The door to my room opened and an older man wearing light blue scrubs walked in.

"You're awake." He smiled. "I'm Dr. Kata, and I dug that nasty bullet out of your shoulder and repaired some artery damage."

"You did an excellent job because I don't feel any pain." I managed a weak smile.

"That's because we have you pumped up on pain meds and a nerve block. Trust me, once it wears off, you'll be cussing me up and down. That sling is to stay on for two weeks. The only time you're allowed to take it off is when you shower. Do you understand me, detective?" His brow arched.

"Yes."

"Also, you are to sleep in a semi-upright position for the next couple of weeks. Do you have an adjustable bed or a recliner?"

"I have a recliner."

"Good. Sleep in that and keep a pillow under that

shoulder for comfort. I've prescribed you some pain medication I'm sending home with you, and an antibiotic. Take the pain meds only if you can't take the pain and finish the round of antibiotics. You're going to need physical therapy which you will start in a couple of weeks. I'm not going to lie to you, it's going to take time to get your arm and shoulder functioning again. But you're in great shape and you're strong, so I do expect a shorter recovery than your average joe."

"What about work?"

He chuckled. "You'll be off at least a month, per me. When your captain decides to let you come back, that's up to him. And when you do go back, it's nothing but light desk duties for a while."

All three of my brothers snickered because they knew me all too well.

"When can I get out of here?"

"In a couple of days. I'll come back in the morning and see how you're doing, check your vitals, and we'll take it from there. In the meantime, you need your rest. You're a lucky man, Detective Kind. The damage could have been much, much worse." He patted my arm before leaving the room.

As soon as the doctor left, my partner, Roman walked in.

"You're awake. Now, I'm going to knock you out for pulling this shit."

"Did you find him?"

"No. Not yet. We checked all his usual hangouts, and he isn't anywhere to be found. He's most likely in hiding."

"Good. Because I want to be the one to find him, and when I do—"

"Relax, partner. We'll get him. Until then, you just focus on getting better."

⁓

"*A*sshole," I heard a whisper in my ear. Opening my eyes, I saw Jenni hovering over me, and a smile crossed my lips.

"Hello to you too."

"Are you an idiot? You could have been killed and then what?"

"I guess you would have to call someone else for a booty call." I gave her a smirk.

Her eyes steadily narrowed at me as her face was mere inches from mine.

"Very funny. Anyway, I'm happy you're okay. I brought you some get-well flowers." She smiled as she pointed to the arrangement sitting on the small table next to the chair.

"Thank you, Jen. That was really sweet of you."

The door to my room opened and Sam and Julia walked in.

"Hey, Simon." Julia walked over and kissed my cheek. "I made you some apple turnovers." She set the container on my tray.

"Thanks, Julia."

"Hey, bro." Sam walked over and held out his fist. "How are you feeling this morning?"

"Not too bad as long as I keep pushing this button to the pain pump."

"You better watch how often you do that." Emilia smiled as she walked in. "It'll run out before you know it, and you won't get another one." She walked over and kissed my cheek. "How are you?"

"I'm good, Emilia. Where's Sebastian?"

"He's on his way with breakfast for you. I have to get to the office, but I wanted to stop by and check on you first." She grabbed hold of my hand.

"Thanks. You didn't have to do that."

"Sure, I did." A smile crossed her lips. "And just so you know, I will be helping you clean that wound and change your bandages when you get home."

"You can be my doctor anytime." I gave her a wink.

"I heard that, douchebag." Sebastian walked into the room. "Say something like that to my girlfriend again, and I'll shoot you in the other arm."

"Ouch, bro. You'd really do that to an already wounded man?"

"You bet I would. I brought you breakfast so you don't have to eat the ungodly stuff they call food in this place."

"You're the best. I love you man."

"Love you too, bro." He grabbed my hand and leaned in for a light hug.

"I need to head out and get ready for a shoot." Jenni smiled as she leaned over and kissed my cheek. "I'll call you later."

"Thanks, Jenni."

As Emilia and Jenni both walked out of the room, Stefan walked in.

"Good morning." He grinned. "Oh hey, did Sebastian make that?" He pointed to my plate.

"Yes."

"Bro?" He cocked his head at our brother.

"Really, Stefan? I cook for you all the time. Are you laying in a hospital bed with a gunshot wound and recovering from surgery?"

"Is that what it's going to take?" Stefan's brow raised.

Sebastian chuckled. "Shut the hell up."

"Lily has a half-day of school today, so Alex said she'll stop by after she picks her up. Lily was crying in the middle of the night because she's so worried about you."

5

"Poor kid. I'm glad Alex is bringing her up so she can see I'm okay."

My brothers and I talked for a while and then they left. I was in more pain than I was letting on and the last thing I wanted was for them to worry about me. They'd been through enough already. My mom and Curtis stopped by for a visit and when they left, my dad walked in.

"How are you, son?"

"I'm okay, Dad."

"You gave us all quite a scare. Celeste and I were talking, and we think you should come and stay with us while you recuperate."

Hell no.

"Thanks, Dad, but I'll be fine at home. Plus, you're only a few houses down if I need anything."

"You shouldn't be alone. Now, if you had someone special in your life—"

"Dad—"

"All I'm saying is you can clearly see how Julia, Alex, and Emilia, make your brothers happy."

"I am happy, Dad. I don't need someone for that, and I'm certainly not putting my happiness in the hands of someone else."

"You're tough son, but underneath all that tough exterior is someone who needs somebody."

"Okay, Dad. If you say so."

I wasn't going to argue with him about it.

"Listen, Dad. I love you, but I'm really tired and I need to go to sleep."

"Sure thing, son. When you're out of here, we're going to have a little chat about a possible career change."

"You know that's a losing battle, so save your breath. I will never give up being a detective."

"A father can try." He sighed.

I turned my head and stared out the window as I thought about last night. How could I have been so stupid not to have seen him? I had better instincts than that. I was going to find him and beat the shit out him until he told me where I could find his boss.

CHAPTER 2

ONE MONTH LATER

*S*imon

"Are you okay, big boy?" Jenni breathlessly asked as her hips grind back and forth on my cock.

"Yeah. I'm good." I threw my head back and let out a groan as she came. Gripping her hips, I held her down and exploded inside her.

She leaned in and brushed her lips against mine before climbing off me.

"Thanks." I grinned as I glanced over her. "I really needed that."

A happy smile crossed her lips. "You're welcome, but I think we should talk." She rolled on her side and ran her finger over my chest.

"About?"

"You are my best guy friend, Simon, and I love you like a best friend. Your friendship is very important to me and as much as it pains me to say this, I don't think we should sleep together anymore."

My lips formed a soft smile as I brought my hand up and stroked her cheek.

"Your friendship is very important to me too, and I don't want to do anything to ever compromise that. So, if you think we should stop, I agree."

"Are you sure?"

"One day, you're going to meet a guy and fall head over heels for him. I want that for you, Jen."

"Same goes for you too, Simon. Except you'll meet an amazing woman."

"Come on. You know me better than that." I smiled.

"Do I really?" Her brow arched.

"You should by now."

"I only know what you want me to know, detective. But I do know deep inside that guarded and locked heart of yours," she placed her hand over my heart, "there is love locked away just waiting for the one woman in this world who was born with the key to unlock it."

Grabbing hold of her hand that laid gently over my heart, I pressed my lips against it.

"That was very poetic, but I like my life the way it is."

"I know you do. But sometimes the universe and fate doesn't give two shits what you like." Her lips formed a pretty smile.

When I awoke the next morning, I gripped my shoulder as I sat up and placed my feet firmly on the floor. It had been four weeks since the shooting and the pain still gripped me. The narcotics the doctor prescribed me were becoming a crutch. One twinge of pain and I was popping them like candy. After making a cup of coffee, I took it outside, walked down to the beach, and planted myself in the sand.

"Hey, bro." Sam walked over and placed his hand on my shoulder.

Looking up at him, I gave him a small smile.

"What's going on? Why are you down here so early?"

"Why are you?" I asked my brother.

"Because I saw you walk down here. How's the shoulder?"

"Hurts like a bitch."

"I saw Jenni leaving your house. Were you guys too rough in the sack?" A smirk crossed his lips.

I let out a chuckle. "Maybe a little. We aren't hooking up anymore. Last night was the last time."

"Music to my ears. But why?"

"We're close friends and we don't want to do anything to jeopardize that."

"How do you really feel about it?"

"I'm good with it. She's important to me, and I value our friendship more than just having an occasional hookup. Besides, I don't want it to be weird for her when she meets the 'one' and we'd just had sex. You know what I mean?"

"Yeah," he placed his hand on my back, "I know what you mean, brother."

~

I lightly knocked on the door before opening it and stepping inside.

"Hey, Captain."

"Kind, come in and have a seat." He motioned with his hand. "How are you doing?"

"I'm doing great, and I'm excited to get back to work."

"I got a call today from Dr. Kazmin, the psychologist you were supposed to set an appointment with and haven't yet." His brow raised.

"Captain, I'm—"

"I don't care, Kind. It's required after a shooting. You know that."

"I know, but I don't need to see her. I'm perfectly fine."

"I was shot once, and I insisted I was fine too. Then one

day I snapped because I wasn't. So, get that goddamn appointment made and get your ass over to see her."

"When can I come back?"

He sat behind his desk and stared at me with that look. The one he always gave when what he had to say wasn't good news.

"Another four weeks."

"Fuck! Captain—"

He put his hand up. "I want you completely healed, Kind. If you want to come back and sit behind the desk, be my guest. But I know you won't. You're one of the best detectives I've had and I'm not compromising that by bringing you back too soon. Consider it a vacation. You're getting paid anyway, so enjoy your time off. And if you do anything stupid while you're on downtime, I'll suspend your ass, and you'll be off even longer. Got it?"

A smirk crossed my lips as I looked at him. "Got it."

He knew me too well and being my captain, he had to warn me.

I walked out of his office and over to Roman's desk.

"What did he say?"

"Another four weeks."

"Shit, man. I'm sorry."

"You have my back, right?" I asked him.

"Of course, I do. Anything you need, you call me."

"Thanks." I placed my hand on his shoulder.

I walked out of the station, climbed in my car, and scoured the hangouts where my CI usually hung out.

"Where is he, Vinnie?" I hastily walked over to him and grabbed him by his shirt.

"Damn, Kind. No need for violence. I heard what happened."

"Where the fuck is he hiding?" My grip on his shirt tightened.

"Okay. Okay." He put his hands up. "Shit. You know they'll kill me if they see me talking to you. You just can't come at me in broad daylight like this, bro."

"Don't you know me by now, Vinnie? Now tell me where he's hiding."

"I already told that partner of yours I don't know."

"Bullshit, Vinnie!" I grabbed his shirt.

His head turned from side to side making sure none of his crew was around.

"Fine. He's held up in an abandoned warehouse over in South Park. Sometimes, I bring him food and shit. He knows the cops are after him for shooting you, so he was told to lay low."

"Which warehouse?"

As soon as he told me, I let go of his shirt.

"Thank you. I don't understand why you have to make things so difficult. You agreed to give me information."

"Only because you're keeping me out of jail."

"And I will continue to do that as long as you cooperate."

"Yeah. Yeah." He smoothed out his shirt. "Next time, call me first so we can meet somewhere more private. You know they'll kill me, Simon."

"I'm not going to let anything happen to you." I smirked as I tapped the side of his head.

"You better hope the hot chick didn't get to him first," he said as I walked away.

Stopping in my tracks, I turned around and furrowed my brows at him.

"What are you talking about? Who?"

"I don't know who she was, but she wanted to know where Cody was."

"Did you tell her?"

"I had no choice, man. She shoved me against the wall and almost broke my arm. I've never seen her before in my life."

"But yet you weren't going to tell me?" I balled my fist as I started walking towards him.

"I was just playing with you, Simon." He put his hands up. "I swear."

I shook my head and headed to my car.

When I pulled up to the warehouse, I saw a shadow black Mustang Shelby GT parked on the side.

"Shit."

Before climbing out of my car, I grabbed my gun and walked around the back of the building. The back door was ajar, so I quietly slipped in.

CHAPTER 3

*G*race
Pulling up to the warehouse, I climbed out of my car and placed my hand on the gun that was secured in my holster. I quietly snuck around the back. If he was in there, he knew I was coming because he would have heard me pull up. Picking the lock on the back door, I carefully opened it and stepped inside. The clicking of my heels against the concrete made it impossible to keep quiet. But I didn't care. I wanted him to know I was coming.

"Who's there?" I heard him shout in the distance as the cocking of his gun made me sigh.

Grabbing my gun from the holster, I held it firmly in my hands as I hid behind a tall steel beam. That's when I felt the tip of his gun touch the back of my head.

"Drop it, bitch, and slowly turn around."

Rolling my eyes, I carefully bent down, placed my weapon on the ground, and slowly turned to face him. He kicked the gun away and then stood there with a smile on his face as his gun pointed directly at my forehead.

"Who the hell are you?" His eyes narrowed. "Wait a minute. You're that cop from New York."

"You tried to kill me."

"You had it coming. That's what happens when you meddle in our affairs. No one gets out alive. Now it looks like I can finish the job." A smug look crossed his face.

"Yeah. I don't think so." I scrunched my face before I wrapped both my hands around his wrist and ducked as the gun went off.

After striking him in the balls, I grabbed his gun and threw it across the warehouse before striking him again. He tried to fight back but I escaped every punch and kick he threw at me. As badly as I wanted to kill him, I needed information first.

"You bitch!" he screamed as I heard the cracking of his arm and he fell to his knees. One swift kick in the jaw and he was down, moaning in pain. Grabbing my gun from the floor, I pressed my heel into his abdomen to keep him down as I pointed it at him.

"Where is Victor Ives?"

"I don't know. I swear I don't. He never tells us his location," he mumbled. "We've never even met him."

"LAPD, drop your weapon!" I heard a voice from behind.

~

*S*imon

"You have got to be kidding me," she said.

"Slowly place your weapon on the ground and kick it across the floor."

She did as I asked.

"With your hands up, slowly step away from him and turn around."

When she turned around, her beauty paralyzed me.

"Who are you?" I asked.

"Can you please stop pointing your gun at me? I'm only here to get some information from this scumbag."

I looked down at Cody who was barely conscious. His face was full of blood, and he was gripping his arm.

"Did you break his arm?"

"Yeah. I did. He had a gun pointed at my forehead."

"It looks like you broke his jaw too."

"He kept calling me a bitch." Her brow arched. "Can you put your gun away? I'm not a threat to you. I just need to know where his boss is hiding."

"Who are you and what do you want with Victor Ives?"

"Tell me who you are first."

"Detective Simon Kind, LAPD."

"Detective Grace Adams, NYPD."

"You're a long way from home, detective. You don't have jurisdiction here."

She cocked her head as a beautiful smile graced her face.

"It's personal, detective. Why are you after him?"

I lowered my gun and put it back in my pocket.

"He shot me a month ago. So, right now, it's personal for me too."

"I'm sorry. If you want to finish him off, go right ahead." She gestured with her hand.

"I think you did a pretty good job." I let out a sigh as I looked down at Cody who was now lying there unconscious.

"I'm on medical leave so I can't call this in."

"Can't I just put a bullet in him? Please." Her lips formed a pout.

"No. You cannot. Is that his gun over there?" I pointed.

"Yeah."

"Wipe it clean, and let's get out of here. As far as I'm concerned neither of us were here. Are you hungry?"

"A little."

"Let's go grab some lunch and talk. Meet me at Four Kinds in Venice Beach. My brother owns the place, and we can talk there in private."

She pulled her phone from her pocket.

"Address?" she asked.

I rattled it off as we both walked out of the warehouse.

"I have someone who will call this in, and I'll meet you at the restaurant. Don't ditch me either." I pointed at her as she opened her car door.

"Are you buying?" She grinned.

"Yeah. I'm buying."

"Then I won't ditch you. I never turn down a free meal." She climbed in her car and shut the door.

I let out a chuckle as I pulled out my phone and dialed Vinnie.

"What now, Kind?" he answered.

"Your boy is down and needs medical attention. Call 911 and give them the address to the warehouse."

"What the fuck did you do?"

"I didn't do anything. The hot chick did. Call it in. I'll be in touch." I ended the call.

I climbed in my car and pulled away. Damn. Sexy wasn't a word that did her justice. Her five-foot-eight lean and ripped body caught my attention very quickly, as did her long dark hair, beautiful green eyes, and full lips that would look amazing wrapped around my cock. She was a very desirable woman, and what she did to Cody was unbelievable. I needed to find out everything I could about her, and I'd give her the chance to tell me over lunch. If I felt she was holding anything back, or lying, I'd investigate Detective Grace Adams myself.

CHAPTER 4

*G*race

His voice from behind was sexy, but when I turned around, my eyes didn't prepare me for what I'd seen. Six foot three inches, short dark hair, hypnotic blue eyes, a neatly trimmed dark beard that sat upon his masculine jawline, and a thin well-kept mustache above his full lips. My eyes mainly stayed focused on his, but they sure noticed his ripped and fit body. I was always a sucker for a man with defined muscles.

I pulled into the parking lot of the restaurant and Simon pulled into the space next to me. Grabbing my purse, I climbed out.

"By the way, nice car." A smile crossed his lips.

"Thanks, it's a rental."

"Shall we?" He gestured with his hand.

When we stepped inside, he led me over to a booth in the corner. A young woman followed us and set two menus down on the table.

"Thanks, Kara."

"You're welcome, Simon. Do you want me to let Sebastian know you're here?"

"He's here? I thought he was at the other restaurant today?"

"He sent Marco over there."

"You might as well. He's going to see me anyway."

"I take it Sebastian is your brother?" I spoke.

"Yeah. He's one of my brothers."

"How many do you have?"

"Three. We're quadruplets."

"Seriously?" I cocked my head. "I've never met anyone who was a quadruplet before."

"A lot of people haven't." The corners of his mouth curved upward.

"Hey, bro. Well, hello there." A handsome man smiled when we walked over.

"This is my brother, Sebastian. Sebastian, meet Detective Grace Adams of the NYPD."

"It's a pleasure to meet you." He extended his hand to me.

"It's a pleasure to meet you as well, Sebastian." I placed my hand in his. "You have a beautiful restaurant."

"Thank you. Did you two order yet?"

"No. Do you know what you want, or do you need some more time?"

"Nope." I grinned. "I'll have the lobster roll with the sweet potato fries."

"Same for me, bro."

"Great. I'll get that ready for you. Beer, wine, cocktail?" Sebastian glanced at me.

"Gin and tonic. It's five o'clock somewhere in the world." I smiled.

"Beer for me," Simon said as he gripped his shoulder.

"Is that where you got shot?"

"Yeah. Four weeks out and it still hurts like a bitch."

"It's going to take time."

"Yeah. Well, I'm not a very patient guy. How are you involved with Ives and his crew?"

"Probably the same reason you are. Illegal gun sales, drugs, murder, sex trafficking."

"I know nothing about the NYPD working with the LAPD on this." His eye steadily narrowed at me.

Sebastian walked over and set our food in front of us.

"Thank you, Sebastian. They're not. But I am." I looked at Simon as I picked up my lobster roll.

"By yourself?"

"Yeah." I slowly nodded and then took a bite.

"Does your captain know?"

"Nope." I shook my head. "She thinks I'm in Cabo."

"So, you came here to take down the syndicate yourself?" His brow raised.

"Pretty much. Anyway, you seem to be working solo. You're on medical leave, yet you showed up at the warehouse by yourself. Does your captain know?" I cocked my head as I picked up a sweet potato fry.

"Well…"

"I take that as a no. So, how are you any different?"

"The difference is I'm a cop here. You're not. You're like a civilian—"

"Finish that sentence, Detective Kind, and I can't be responsible for what I might do to you."

He let out a chuckle. "You can't do that, and you can't say shit like that. Especially to me."

"And why is that?"

"Because it's hot and it turns me on. So, just stop."

I sat there for a moment and narrowed my eyes at him before a smile crossed my lips.

"Fair enough. But I'm not leaving L.A. until I get every one of them."

CHAPTER 5

*S*imon

During our conversation, my phone kept blowing up. When I pulled it from my pocket, I had several text messages from my two brothers in our group chat.

"Bro, who's the hot chick?" Stefan texted.

"Sebastian said she's a detective from New York. Why is she here?" Sam asked.

"Where did you find her?" Stefan again.

"Are we interrupting something?" Sam asked.

"Lunch at the restaurant?. You wanted us to know." Stefan said.

"Knock it off, bros! I'll talk to you all later tonight. My house at seven o'clock."

"So, where are you staying while you're in town?" I asked Grace.

My phone rang and when I looked over at it, I saw Roman was calling.

"Hold on." I held my finger up to Grace. "Hey, Roman."

"Hey. Our boy Cody was found."

"Really? Where?"

"In a warehouse in South Park. He was badly beaten. His arm is broken and so is his jaw. He's in the hospital and he's still unconscious. You wouldn't happen to know anything about that, would you?"

"No. How would I know? And even if I did find him, I couldn't have done that to him with my shoulder. Someone else got to him." My eyes diverted to Grace.

"We're just waiting for him to wake up to question him."

"Okay. Let me know."

"I will, partner. Talk to you later."

I set down my phone and sighed.

"Your partner?" Grace asked.

"Yeah. Cody is still unconscious. You didn't answer my question. Where are you staying?"

"Days Inn. Anyway, thanks for lunch. I need to get going."

"You're welcome. Hand me your phone." I held out my hand, palm facing up.

"Why?"

"I'm going to put in my number. I want you to have it if you need anything."

She took her phone from her purse and handed it to me. After I put in my number, I sent myself a text message. When my phone lit up, she glanced over at it and then looked back at me as I sat there with a smile on my face.

"I can't believe I fell for that." She shook her head.

"Will you promise me something?" I asked her.

"What?"

"If you find out anything, I need you to call me. Promise?"

"Yeah. I'll call you."

She slid out of the booth, and I walked her to the door.

"Be careful, Grace," I spoke with a serious tone.

"You don't have to worry about me, detective. I can take care of myself."

"I have no doubt you can but promise me you'll still be

careful."

"I will." A small smile crossed her lips.

As soon as she walked out, I went to the kitchen to say goodbye to Sebastian.

"I'm heading out, bro. Thanks for lunch. By the way, be at my house tonight at seven. Bring the food."

"Hold on a second. What's going on with that woman?"

"We'll talk later. I have to go."

I thought about Grace the rest of the day. No matter what I did, I couldn't get her out of my head. I still had so many questions for her. She said going after Ives was personal, but she wouldn't say why. Taking a seat at my computer in my home office, I ran a search on her. Leaning back in my chair, I placed my hands behind my head and stared at the screen.

"Who the hell are you really, Grace Adams?"

"Bro?" Stefan interrupted my thoughts. "What are you doing? We're all outside."

"Sorry. I didn't realize the time."

"Sam brought the beer."

I followed my brother outside and saw Sam and Sebastian sitting down in the loungers. Sam grabbed a beer bottle from the case and held it out to me.

"Thanks." I took a seat next to him.

"So, are you going to tell us who the hot chick is?" Stefan asked with a grin on his face.

Taking the cap off the bottle, I flung it at him.

"Her name is Grace Adams and she's a detective with the NYPD."

"How did you meet up with her?" Sam's brows furrowed. "You're not even working right now."

I brought the bottle up to my lips and took a sip.

"I found my CI earlier and he told me where Cody was."

"The guy who shot you?" Sebastian's brows furrowed.

"Yes. When I got to the warehouse, he was lying on the floor all beat to shit with a broken arm and broken jaw. Grace had the heel of her shoe jammed into his abdomen while holding her gun to him."

"Holy shit!" Stefan laughed. "Are you serious? She did all that to the guy?"

"She did, and she doesn't have a scratch on her."

"I think the important question here is what the hell were you doing going to that warehouse when you're on leave?" Sam asked.

"Come on, bro. You already know the answer to that," Sebastian spoke.

"So, what is Grace doing here? How did she find this guy?"

"She told me she's after Ives and his crew for 'personal' reasons. Apparently, she tracked down my CI and made him tell her."

"And that's all you know?" Sam asked.

"She said she isn't leaving L.A. until she gets every last one of them."

"Damn. I want to meet her," Stefan said.

"She's hot, bro." Sebastian grinned at him.

"Where is she now?" Sam asked.

"I don't know. She left after lunch. I gave her my number and I got hers. I made her promise to call me if she finds out anything."

"What does she look like?" Stefan asked.

"She's tall, lean, but kind of built, green eyes, long dark hair," Sebastian said.

"Really?" I cocked my head at him and narrowed my eyes.

"What? He asked and I answered."

"I'm telling Emilia you're checking out other women." I pointed my finger at him.

"Please. I wasn't checking her out. Besides, Emilia will always be the most beautiful woman in the world to me."

"Why are you getting all worked up?" Stefan asked.

"I'm not getting worked up. What the fuck?" I held out my arms.

"Yes, you are." A smirk crossed Sam's lips.

"The hell I am. You shouldn't be talking about other women like that."

"Really?" Sebastian cocked his head at me. "Didn't you tell Emilia that she could be your doctor any day?"

"And? I'm not in a relationship. The three of you are!"

As we were sitting there talking, Julia walked over and sat down on Sam's lap.

"How's your shoulder, Simon?"

"It hurts, Julia. But I'll be fine. How are you feeling?"

"Sick as usual." A soft smile crossed her lips. "Don't forget that I have my doctor's appointment in the morning," she said to Sam.

"I haven't forgotten, baby." He kissed her head. "You look tired. Let's go home. It's been fun, my brothers. I'll talk to you three tomorrow."

"Good night, Sam. Good night, Julia," the three of us spoke at the same time.

"Have you guys noticed that Julia is already starting to show?" I asked. "She isn't that far along."

"Emilia made a comment about that the other day and said that it's possible she's carrying twins since they run in Julia's family," Sebastian said.

"Shit. I didn't even think of that." Stefan laughed. "Oh my God, Sam would die. Double the mess."

Sebastian and I started laughing with him. When my phone rang, I pulled it from my pocket and saw it was Grace.

CHAPTER 6

*G*race

I stood in the middle of my motel room and stared at the two guys lying unconscious on the floor. Bringing my hand up to my forehead, I wiped the blood that ran down the side of my face. Grabbing my phone, I took pictures, took their phones from their pockets, unlocked them with their faces, and then I climbed into my car and sped away, making sure I wasn't being followed. I pulled over in a parking lot and called Simon.

"Hey. What's up?"

"My motel room is trashed, and two guys are lying on the floor unconscious." I sent him the pictures.

"Jesus Christ. Are you okay?"

"I'm fine."

"Are those Ives' guys?"

"Yeah. Two of his goons."

"How did they know where you were staying?"

"I think they followed me from the hospital."

"What? Why the hell would you go there?"

"To see our friend."

"Where are you now?"

"In a parking lot."

"I'm sending you my address right now. You'll stay at my place tonight and we can talk."

"Simon, I don't—"

"It's not up for debate, Grace. Just get here as fast as you can and when you get here, come around the back."

As I was about to say something, I heard a click. Looking at my text messages, I punched his address into the GPS and headed to his house. I parked the car down the street, grabbed my bag, and walked until I found his house. He told me to come around the back and when I did, I saw Simon and two other men sitting on the patio with a fire going in the firepit. When Simon saw me, he jumped up from his chair.

"You're bleeding." He walked over to me.

"I'm fine."

"I'll go get Emilia," Sebastian said.

Simon lightly took hold of my arm. "Let's get you inside."

We stepped through the door and inside the kitchen where I sat down at the table. Simon grabbed a cloth and handed it to me.

"Grace, this is my brother Stefan."

"It's nice to meet you." I smiled. "What a first impression I must be making."

"Nah. You're good." Stefan gave me a wink. "We don't judge here."

Sebastian and a woman, whom I presumed was Emilia, stepped through the door. She walked over and set her black bag on the table.

"Hi." She smiled. "I'm Emilia. Let me take a look."

"I'm fine. Simon is overreacting. It's nice to meet you. I'm Grace."

I lowered the cloth from my head.

"Good news is all you need is a butterfly bandage. Let's get this cleaned up first. It's going to hurt a little bit. Let me know when you're ready."

Simon walked over with a glass of scotch and set it down in front of me.

"You're probably going to need this first." A smirk crossed his lips.

"Thanks." I threw the golden liquid down my throat until the glass was empty. "Okay. I'm ready."

Emilia poured some cleaner on a large cotton pad and pressed it against my wound as I took in a deep breath.

"You took down three guys in a matter of hours," Simon said. "How did you not know they were following you?"

"Apparently, they did a good job of not being seen. I took their phones and unlocked them. They're in my bag over there."

"All set." Emilia smiled after she placed the butterfly bandage over my wound.

"Thank you. I take it you're a doctor?"

"A pediatrician."

"Thank you again."

"You're welcome. You might want to take some Motrin for the pain and get some rest."

"I will."

"We're going to head home, bro, and let the two of you talk," Sebastian said.

"It was nice to meet you, Grace," Emilia spoke.

"Yeah. It was a pleasure." The corners of Stefan's mouth curved upward.

"It was nice to meet all of you. I'm sorry it wasn't under better circumstances."

After they left, Simon poured me another drink and sat down across from me.

"You did make sure the location was turned off on both their phones, right?" he asked.

"Of course."

"Okay. I'll run the phone numbers through my computer. Have you ever seen them before?"

"I did once in a club back in New York."

"Looking at the pictures you sent, the damage to your room is extensive. That must have been some fight. The police are going to want to talk to you."

"I registered the room under an alias, and paid cash for the month. They won't be able to trace it back to me."

"Smart woman." He smiled. "I put your bag in my guest room. If you want to take a bath, there's a jet tub in the guest bathroom. But be careful not to get your cut wet."

"I know. This isn't my first wound, detective." I smiled.

"I'm sure it isn't."

"A hot bath does sound amazing right now."

"Then go take one. Your room is up the stairs and the second door on the right. When you're done, come outside on the patio."

"Thanks for inviting me to stay the night. I could have just gone to another motel."

"I feel better knowing you're safe here." A small smile formed on his lips.

"I can take care of myself."

"Oh, trust me, I know that. Go take your bath." He gave me a wink as he got up from his seat.

CHAPTER 7

Grace

The intense attraction I'd felt towards him was unnerving. It was good to see him again all grown up. He was sexy as sin, and he was genuinely nice. Just like he was all those years ago. I needed to be careful because I didn't want him getting hurt. That was the problem with me. Everyone I was close to ended up dead. But I was going to put a stop to it once I found Victor Ives and killed him myself.

After my bath, I threw on a pair of leggings and a sweat-shirt. As I stared at myself in the mirror, I took my hair out of the messy bun I'd had it in and pulled it back into a pony-tail. When I stepped outside on the patio, I took a seat in the lounger next to Simon.

"How was your bath?"

"It was great. Thank you."

"Sebastian sent over a charcuterie board." He picked it up from the side table and handed it to me.

"Wow. That was so nice of him. Your brothers seem really great. I take it they live close?"

"They are great and yes," he smirked, "see these houses? Sam, Stefan, Sebastian, and then my father and Celeste live in the house next to Sebastian."

"Oh." My brows raised with surprise.

"Right?" He chuckled. We weren't prepared when he announced he was buying the house and moving in. The house belonged to Emilia. Then she moved in with Sebastian and my father bought it from her."

"I take it Celeste isn't your mother?"

"She's my fourth step-mother." He slowly shook his head. "He's on his fifth marriage. But wait, it gets better."

"It does?" I grinned.

"Celeste is pregnant."

"What?" I scrunched my face. "How old is she?"

"She's forty-two."

"Okay. Okay." I slowly nodded my head. "And you're what? Early thirties?"

"Thirty-three."

"So, when your new brother or sister is twenty, you'll be in your fifties." I laughed.

"Yeah. Old enough to be the kid's father. Can I get you a glass of wine or another scotch?"

"I'll take a glass of wine, if you don't mind."

"What color? Wait, let me guess. You're a white wine kind of girl."

"Very good, detective."

"I'll be right back."

I sat there grazing on some cheese and crackers while I stared out at the dark water and listened to the rustling of the waves.

"Again, Grace."

"I can't."

"You can and you will. You will work on it again and again

31

until you master it. I'm going inside. You stay and practice. Listen to the ocean as it speaks to you. Concentrate, Grace."

"Are you okay?"

"Yeah." I glanced over at him as he handed me a glass of wine. "Thanks."

"You looked like you were zoned out."

"I was just listening to the waves." I smiled.

"Where did you learn to fight?"

I knew that question was coming sooner or later.

"I just picked up some things here and there."

He stared at me for a moment as if he didn't believe me.

"There's one thing I want to make very clear to you, Grace. There are no lies allowed here. Your captain thinks you're in Cabo on vacation, you came to California for personal reasons having to do with Victor Ives and his crew, and your fighting skills are impeccable from what I can tell just by the fact you took down three men today on your own. If you want my help, you better be straight with me."

"I didn't ask you for your help, Simon. But if you really want to know, my name is Grace Elizabeth Adams. I was born and raised in Salt Lake City Utah, my parents are John and Deborah Adams, and I'm an only child."

"The one thing that makes me such a good detective is the fact that I have excellent instincts. And right now, my instincts are telling me you're still lying. And another thing, if you didn't want my help, you never would have called me after you took down those two men in your motel room."

"Listen, we're both after the same people," I said. "Let's just focus on that."

"I'm after them because it's my job and my case. We need to get these assholes to save people's lives. For you it's personal, and I want to know why."

"And I'll tell you when I feel like I can trust you."

"You don't trust me right now?" His brows furrowed and

I looked away from him. "Well guess what, sweetheart, I don't trust you either."

"Fine." I set my glass of wine down. "Then I'll leave."

I got up from my chair and stormed into the house.

"You're not going anywhere. It's late and you're tired." He followed behind me as I ran up the stairs.

Grabbing my bag, I threw it over my shoulder and stood in front of him as he blocked the doorway to the bedroom.

"Get out of my way, Simon."

"I'm afraid I can't do that. Put your bag down."

"You really want to do this?" I slowly shook my head. "You have a hurt shoulder as it is."

"You wouldn't dare. I'm not the bad guy here. All I want is for you to tell me the truth about who you really are."

"I already told you. Now, please move out of the way."

"No. You'll have to go through me if you want to leave." His dreamy eyes stared into mine.

"What the hell is wrong with you, Kind?"

"What the hell is wrong with you, Adams?"

"How will I know if I can trust someone, uncle?"

"You will feel it from within, my darling. Look into their eyes and let your heart guide you, even if your mind is fighting you."

I trusted him then and my heart told me I could trust him now.

"Grace?" I heard Simon's voice that snapped me back into the present.

I diverted my eyes to his and stared into them for a moment.

"Fine. You win." I set my bag down. "We'll talk in the morning. I'm tired and would like to go to sleep."

"Okay. Just so you know, I'm setting the house alarm. So, if you try to leave, I'll know." A smirk crossed his lips.

"I'm too tired to even try and leave, both physically and mentally."

He brought his thumb up to my forehead and lightly stroked the area around my cut.

"Do you want to take anything for this?"

"No. I'm fine." I could feel myself tremble underneath his touch.

"Okay. Get some rest. I'll see you in the morning." The corners of his mouth curved upward.

"You too, Simon," I spoke in a soft voice.

As soon as he turned and walked away, I shut the door and softly placed my forehead against it.

CHAPTER 8

$\mathcal{S}$imon

I went downstairs, cleaned up, set the alarm, and headed up to bed. Before I made it to my bedroom, I stopped in the hallway and stared at the door to the guest bedroom. There was something about her I couldn't shake. She was tough—one of the toughest women I'd ever met in my life. But underneath that tough exterior was a broken girl. I could feel it.

My phone pinged in my hand and when I looked at it, I had a message from Sam in our chat group.

"I heard you have an overnight guest. I'm sorry I missed meeting her. But don't worry, I'll be over in the morning before we leave for the doctor's appointment."

"She seems really nice, bro. She's beautiful too," Stefan said.

I shook my head as I stepped into my bedroom and shut the door.

"Are you behaving yourself over there?" Sebastian asked.

"You all need to stop. Signing off. I'll talk to you nosey douchebags in the morning. And by the way, not a word of this to

Dad. If you do, I'll have Grace kick your asses." I sent the smiley emoji.

I climbed into bed and took in a deep breath as I held my shoulder. Grabbing the pill bottle from the nightstand, I only had two pills left with no refills. Shit. I shoved it in my mouth and chased it down with the bottle of water I had sitting next to me. Just as I was about to turn off the light, my phone rang and Roman was calling.

"Hey, Roman."

"I thought you'd want to know two more of Victor's guys are in the hospital."

"Damn. Really?"

"Yeah. We found them unconscious in one of the rooms at a Days Inn. The clerk at the desk said he received calls from some of the other guests that there was a lot of fighting going on. So, he went to the room, found them, and called 911. The room is registered under the name of Sylvia Torres. The clerk said she paid cash for the entire month. We're running a check on her now. You don't know her, do you?"

"No. I've never heard that name before. Keep me posted if you find something out."

"I will. I'll talk to you later, partner."

The following morning, I got up, slipped on a pair of pajama bottoms, and headed down for a much-needed cup of coffee. When I made it to the kitchen, I stopped and narrowed my eyes when I saw Grace sitting out on the patio sipping on a cup of coffee.

"Good morning. You're up early," I spoke as I stepped outside.

"Morning. I couldn't sleep."

"I hope it wasn't the bed. I paid top dollar for that mattress." I gave her a smirk.

"No. The bed is very comfortable."

"May I ask how you disabled my security system?"

She glanced over at me with an arch in her brow, a smirk on her face, and didn't say a word.

"Right." I slowly nodded my head as I gripped my shoulder and rubbed it. "My partner Roman called to tell me that the two men you knocked out last night are in the hospital. He's running a check on Sylvia Torres."

"He won't find anything on her." She brought her cup up to her lips.

"I didn't think so." I let out a sigh. "I'm going to make a cup of coffee and take a shower. When I'm done, we're going to talk. Understand?"

With the slight turn of her head, our eyes locked onto each other's.

"I understand."

"Good." I reached over and gave her arm a gentle squeeze before I went inside.

≈

*G*race

I'd inhaled a sharp breath when Simon walked out onto the patio in nothing but a pair of pajama bottoms. From his well-defined upper body down to his washboard abs, and the sexy V-line that was sculpted where his lower abs and obliques met, left me breathless. I needed to tame the dirty thoughts that ran through my head.

When he went to take a shower, I walked down to the beach and nestled myself in the sand into a Sukhasana position to get in some morning meditation. Suddenly, I heard a voice next to me.

"Who are you?"

Opening one eye, I glanced over at the little girl with the long blonde hair staring at me.

"I'm Grace. Who are you?"

"Lily."

"Good morning, Lily. It's nice to meet you." I gave her a warm smile.

"What happened to your head?"

"I fell yesterday."

"Did you have a sleepover with my Uncle Simon?"

"Um…well—he was kind enough to let me stay in his guestroom."

"He has a lot of sleepovers."

"Is that so?" I cocked my head at her as a smile crossed my lips.

"Yeah. My Aunt Jenni is over his house a lot. They don't think I notice, but I do."

"Your Aunt Jenni?"

"She's really not my aunt, but I call her that. See, my Uncle Sam is married to my Aunt Julia and my Aunt Jenni is Aunt Julia's twin sister."

"I see. And who is your dad?"

"Stefan. Alex is my mom. Well, my stepmom, but I consider her my real mom. She used to be my nanny and my dad fell in love with her. She got pregnant with my brother Henry and then they got married."

"Wow. That's great. You got a new mom and a baby brother."

"Lily, who is your new friend?" An older man walked over.

"Hi, Grandpa. This is Grace. She had a sleepover at Uncle Simon's."

Oh my God. Seriously, kid.

"Is that so? Hello, Grace. I'm Henry, Simon's father." He extended his hand.

"It's nice to meet you, Henry." I lightly shook his hand.

"Lily, why don't you run up to the house. Grandma Celeste is making a fresh batch of blueberry muffins."

"Okay, Grandpa. Bye, Grace." She waved.

"Bye, Lily. It was nice to meet you. We didn't have a sleep-over like you think. Your son was kind enough to let me stay in his guestroom last night. We're working on a case together."

"No need to explain, darling." He put his hand up. "So, you're a detective with the LAPD as well?"

"No. I actually work for the NYPD. I'm just here following a case."

"I see. What happened?" He pointed to my head.

"It's no big deal. I fell."

"Dad, what's going on?" A handsome man walked over with his hands tucked into his pants pockets.

"I'm just having a chat with Grace here. She's a friend of Simon's."

"Yes. We've met. Actually, that's why I came out here. Simon asked me to come get you. He needs to speak with you."

"Oh. Okay." I stood up. "It was nice to meet you, Henry."

"It was my pleasure, darling. I hope to see you around more often." He smiled.

As we started to walk away, he lightly placed his hand on my upper back.

"I'm Simon's other brother, Sam. I figured you needed rescuing. My father can be quite inquisitive."

"Thank you. It's nice to meet you, Sam."

He opened the sliding door and we both stepped inside.

"Hey," Simon said as he walked into the kitchen.

"I just rescued her from Dad."

"Oh shit. Thanks, bro." They fist-bumped. "Good luck with the ultrasound. You better call me and let me know how it went."

"I will."

"You and your wife are having a baby?" I smiled at him.

"We are. Our first ultrasound is today."

"That's great. Congratulations."

"Thank you. Well, I better head back. It was great to meet you, Grace. I'll see you, bro."

"Breakfast?" Simon asked as he took out the carton of eggs from the refrigerator.

"Sure. Thanks." I took a seat at the island. "While I was down at the beach, I met your niece, Lily."

"Oh yeah?" He turned and gave me a smile. "She's a great kid."

"Yeah. She's adorable. She asked if we had a sleepover."

"Shit. What did you tell her?"

"I told her you were kind enough to let me stay in your guestroom."

"Good answer." He cracked several eggs into a bowl.

"She told me you have a lot of sleepovers." My lips formed a smirk.

"Did she now?" He let out a sigh, and I laughed.

"Kids see everything. Even if you don't think they do."

"I know. Stefan is so protective of her too. He tries to shield her from everything."

"Well, Stefan seems like a great dad, but no matter how hard a parent tries, it's impossible."

CHAPTER 9

$\mathcal{S}$imon

As I was making the eggs, there was a knock at the front door. Glancing over at my security screen in the kitchen, I saw it was Roman.

"Shit. That's my partner. Just act casual."

"Hey, Roman. Come on in. I'm making some eggs. Do you want some?"

"I'm good, bro." He followed me into the kitchen and stopped when he saw Grace sitting there.

"Roman, this is Grace. Grace, my partner Roman."

"It's nice to meet you, Grace."

"You too, Roman." She gave him a beautiful smile.

I placed some eggs on a plate and set it down in front of her.

"Thanks. I'm going to take this outside on the patio." She picked up her plate and got up from her stool.

"Damn, Simon. She's fucking hot. Where did you meet her?"

"We met at a bar last night."

"And she's still here?" His eye narrowed. "I'm surprised. Usually, you have them out the door before the sun rises."

"Well, she's kind of special. Are you sure you don't want any eggs?"

"No. Thanks. We tried to pull the camera footage from the motel on the day Sylvia Torres checked in."

"And?"

"The footage was somehow erased. And when I ran a check on her, she was as clean as a whistle. This doesn't make any sense. So, I checked the street cam footage and ran the plates on a car that was seen pulling out of the motel last night. Turns out it's a rental from Enterprise and it's rented to a Sylvia Torres."

"Hmm. Have you located the car?" I made him a cup of coffee and handed it to him.

"See, here's the weird thing." He wiggled his finger. "When I was driving down your street, I saw that same car parked several houses down. How weird is that?"

Shit.

"So weird, bro. Wow. Did you check the car?"

"No. But imagine my surprise when I walked in here and saw that beautiful woman, the same woman who was in the car, with a butterfly bandage across her head as if she was just in a fight, sitting right here in my partner's kitchen."

I let out a breath as I stood there and rubbed the back of my neck.

"She's a detective with the NYPD."

"What?" His brows furrowed.

"Listen, Roman, you can't tell anyone about her. Not yet anyway. I met her yesterday at the warehouse where Cody was hiding out."

"She did that to him?"

"Yeah. And the two guys in the motel room."

"Simon, my God."

"She's after Ives and all she told me was that it's personal."

"She just can't go around putting people in the hospital. Fuck." He placed his hands on his head. "Do you know what will happen if anyone finds out about this?"

"No one is going to find out, are they?" I asked in a stern voice.

I walked over to the sliding door and asked Grace to come inside.

"He knows," I said. "He saw your car parked down the street. You can trust him, Grace. He's my partner and we protect each other. Don't we, Roman?"

He placed his hands on his hips as he stood there and stared at her.

"Simon told me you're going after Ives."

"I am."

"Why?"

"It's personal, Roman."

"Do you have any idea how dangerous that man is?"

"Oh, I know. Trust me. But I will bury that son-of-a-bitch, and I'll make sure the LAPD gets the glory of closing the case."

"Roman, come on. I need you to have my back on this," I said. "We need to get Ives, his men, his guns, and his drugs off the streets. Too many people are dying because of him. We've been after this guy for almost a year. Grace can help us."

"And if she gets killed in the process?" He cocked his head.

"I'm not going to get killed," she spoke.

"You can't guarantee that, but fine. As far as I'm concerned, Grace is just a chick you brought home from the bar."

"Thank you, Roman." She gave him a small smile.

"You won't be thanking me if I have to put you in a body

bag." He shook his head. "Thanks for the coffee but I need to get to the station."

As soon as he left, Grace looked at me with furrowed brows.

"Is he always that dramatic?"

"Yeah. Sometimes." I smirked. "Now, we're going to sit down and you're going to tell me everything about you." I gripped my shoulder and slowly closed my eyes.

"We will, but first let me help your shoulder."

"What? If you're trying to stall—"

"I'm not. Just sit down and I'll be right back."

CHAPTER 10

*G*race

    I grabbed the large amber colored bottle from my bag and took it downstairs. When I stepped into the kitchen, Simon was leaning up against the counter with his arms folded.

"Take off your shirt."

"No problem." He grinned as he pulled it off his muscular body.

I swallowed hard as I felt my legs tighten.

"Are any of your brothers around?"

"For what?" His brows furrowed.

"I'm going to need someone to hold you down. If they're not, I can ask your dad."

"Oh, hell no. And why do they have to hold me down? What are you going to do to me?"

"I'm not going to lie, Simon. It's going to hurt, and I can't have you flailing around."

He pointed his finger at me. "You can forget it."

"Do you want to heal faster?" I cocked my head at him. "Or do you want your mind to always think you're in pain and crave those pain pills you take? But hey, if you want to become a pill popping junkie, that's none of my business." I raised my brows and began to walk away.

"Wait. Sebastian is home."

"Dial him and put him on speaker."

He grabbed his phone from the counter and called Sebastian.

"Hey, bro."

"Can you—"

"Hey, Sebastian, it's Grace. Can you come over? I want to help Simon out with his shoulder, and I need you to hold him down while I do that."

"Are you serious? I'll be right over." He laughed.

"Thanks a lot." Simon narrowed his eyes at me.

Within seconds both Sebastian and Stefan stepped through the sliding door.

"Why aren't you at work?" Simon asked.

"When I dropped Lily off at school, I realized I left my phone at home. When I pulled in the driveway, Sebastian was outside and asked me to come over so he could give me a couple things Alex wanted. I'm going to be late, and I don't care. I wouldn't miss this for nothing." He pulled out his phone and held it up.

"Put your fucking phone away. You are not videoing this!"

I let out a snicker.

"Actually, two will work even better. Now, go lay down on the area rug in the living room."

He shot me a dirty look.

Once he was down, Sebastian got on one side of him, and Stefan was on the other side.

"I need you both to hold down his arms and legs."

"Shit. I need Alex over here videoing this." Stefan grinned.

"Call or text her and you die, bro. YOU DIE!"

46

"Dude, you're such an asshole. If this is going to hurt, I'm happy. I hope you feel all the pain."

Sebastian let out a laugh.

I coated my hands with the oil and got down on my knees behind him.

"Are you ready?"

"Just do it and get it over with."

"Hold him down," I spoke to his brothers.

I placed one hand on the front of his shoulder over his bullet wound and my other hand evenly on the backside. Closing my eyes for a moment, I squeezed as hard as I could.

"FUCK!" He let out a shrieking scream as his brothers held him down.

I manipulated the area with my hands as his voice grew louder and he tried his hardest to get out of the grips of his brothers.

"What the hell is going on?" A woman came running into the room holding a baby.

"Babe, you don't want to be here for this. Go back home," Stefan said. "By the way, this is Grace. Grace, this is my wife, Alex, and my son, Henry."

"Nice to meet you." I gave her a small smile as I gripped Simon's shoulder. "Okay. That should do it."

I slowly removed my hands from his shoulder and placed them at the base of his skull and slowly massaged it.

"Calm down. Breathe in, breathe out. You can let go of him now." I looked at his brothers.

"Damn. That was intense," Sebastian said as he stood up.

"I'm sorry, bro," Stefan spoke as he placed his hand on his arm. "Are you okay?"

"Let's help him up to the couch," I said.

"He isn't saying anything. Is he in shock or something?" Sebastian asked.

"He just needs to rest for a few minutes. He'll be fine."

After his brothers and Alex left, I sat down next to Simon on the couch and lightly placed my hand on his arm. He pulled it away and shot me a dirty look.

"Do you know that what you did to me hurt worse than being fucking shot?" he shouted.

"You don't need to shout." I furrowed my brows.

"Yes, Grace! Yes, I do!"

"You'll thank me later."

"Somehow I doubt it." He got up from the couch and went upstairs.

Sighing, I got up and walked down to the beach. After nestling myself in the warm sand, I brought my knees up to my chest, and the memories of that day filled my mind.

"You stole my wave!" he shouted.

"I know and I'm not sorry about it. It was a good wave."

"Wow. Really?" He shook his head.

I laughed as I took my board out of the water.

"You know that was really rude and disrespectful." He followed me.

"Stop following me."

"No. Not until I get an apology. Do you think just because you're a girl, I'm going to let it go?"

I stopped in the sand, set my surfboard down, and stared into his blue eyes, as a feeling erupted in my belly.

"You're right. It was rude and disrespectful, and I'm sorry I stole your wave."

"Thank you. By the way, I was watching you. You're really good."

"Thanks." I bashfully smiled.

"I'm Simon."

"I'm Gr—Renee."

"Are you here alone?" he asked.

"No. My uncle is over there." I pointed. "You?"

"Yeah. Two of my brothers are sick and my other brother is at

work with my dad. My house is only a ten-minute walk from here. Do you want to take our boards back in the water?"

"I would like that, but I have to ask my uncle first. I'll be right back."

I ran over to my uncle and as I approached him, he lowered his sunglasses and looked at me.

"Who is that boy you were talking to?"

"His name is Simon. Can I please hang out with him for a while? Please."

"I don't think it's a good idea, sweetheart."

"Please, Uncle Aiko. Please."

"Fine, Grace. I'm going to head back to the room."

"Thank you." I threw my arms around him.

I ran over to Simon, and we put our boards back in the water. We did more talking than we did surfing. When we were finished, we sat down next to each other in the sand as the warmth of the sun comforted us.

"Are you from around here?" he asked.

"No. My uncle had a funeral to attend. We're leaving tomorrow morning."

"You live with your uncle or something? Where are your parents?"

"They're dead."

"Oh. I'm sorry. So, you live with just your uncle?"

"Yeah. He took me in after my parents died."

"How did they die? Car accident?"

"House fire." I looked down.

"I'm sorry, Renee. I shouldn't have asked."

"No. It's fine."

"Six months ago, my best friend was murdered. I don't like to talk about it, but," he shrugged his shoulders, "I feel like I can talk about it with you."

"I'm sorry, Simon. Do they know who did it?"

"Not yet. They haven't found him. I don't even know if they're

49

trying anymore." He looked down.

"I'm sure they are." I reached over and placed my hand on his arm.

"I go to the police station once a week and talk to the detective who's working the case. They have nothing. No clues, not a shred of evidence, nothing. There's too much bad shit that happens here. Too many murders that don't get solved and murderers who don't get caught. But I'm going to change that."

"How?"

"I'm going to become a cop, and if Drew's killer isn't caught by then, I'm going to find him myself, and I won't stop until I do. Even if it takes me a whole lifetime. I'm not sure I'll ever get over his death."

"A broken mirror cannot shine."

"What?" he asked.

"You're the mirror, Simon, and you're broken into tiny little pieces. As long as you stay that way and focus on the bad, your judgement will always be clouded, and you will never shine. You need to make peace with his death. It's only after you make peace with it your mind can calm, and the road of your journey will be paved with clarity. That's what I had to do with my parent's deaths."

He reached over and placed his hand on mine.

"Is your road paved with clarity?"

"Yes. It is."

"I wish you weren't leaving tomorrow," he spoke. "I kind of like hanging out and talking to you." The corners of his mouth curved up into a shy smile.

"I like hanging out and talking to you too, Simon."

"Sweetheart, it's time to come now." I heard my uncle's voice shout from behind.

"I have to go." I got up from the sand and dusted myself off.

"Wait. How can I get in touch with you?"

"You can't. Maybe one day we'll meet again. Goodbye, Simon."

CHAPTER 11

*S*imon
       I sat on the edge of my bed as I began to calm down. I shouldn't have shouted at Grace the way I did, but it couldn't be helped. I had a high pain tolerance, but that was something I never wanted to experience again.

Getting up from my bed, I walked over to the window and saw her sitting down by the water. I supposed I owed her an apology, even though she didn't deserve one after what she'd done to me. I was never going to hear the end of this from my brothers. Grabbing my phone from my dresser, I saw I had a text message from Sam in our group chat.

"We had the ultrasound, and Julia and I want everyone to come over tonight. Simon, you can invite Grace if she's still there."

"Is everything okay?" I asked.

"Yeah. Everything is good. We just want our family with us tonight. We have pictures."

"Emilia and I will be there."

"We'll be there too." Stefan texted. *"I'm not too sure Grace will still be around. I'm sure Simon kicked her out already."*

"Very funny, douchebag. We'll be there, Sam."

After grabbing a bottle of water from the refrigerator, I walked down to the beach and planted myself in the sand next to Grace.

"I see you survived." She smirked.

"Very funny. I'm sorry for shouting at you the way I did."

"Apology accepted." She nudged my good shoulder.

"What are you doing out here?" I asked.

With the slight turn of her head, she stared at me for a moment.

"You don't remember me, do you?"

"Uh, what do you mean?"

Shit. Did I fuck her one time while I was wasted and don't remember? No way. I would never have forgotten that no matter how drunk I was.

"Was Drew's killer ever found?"

"How do you know about Drew?" I narrowed my eyes at her.

"You told me. You also told me that you weren't sure if you'd ever get over his death."

"That's impossible. There was only one person I ever said those words to, and her name was Renee."

The corners of her mouth curved upward into a beautiful smile as I stared into her green eyes. The same green eyes I stared into twenty years ago.

"My God. It can't be. Renee?" My brows furrowed.

"Yeah. It's me, Simon. The same thirteen-year-old girl who stole your wave."

"What the—"

"I know. Crazy, right?"

"I'm totally confused here."

"My birth name is Renee Avery Fuller, but she died in the house fire with her parents."

"I don't understand."

"My parents were murdered, Simon. And as far as

52

everyone is concerned, their ten-year-old daughter died with them in that fire."

"Jesus Christ, Grace. Who would do that?"

"Ives."

"What?" I frowned in confusion.

"Not Victor Ives, but by his father, Edwardo. He killed my parents and he tried to kill me."

"I'm sorry. I had no—"

"It's fine."

"I have to ask you this, and I'm not quite sure how."

"I know what you're going to ask and no, my parents weren't criminals. They were both highly trained and highly ranked undercover FBI agents. After they arrested Ives and sent him to prison, they received threating emails and pictures of me someone had taken. They were from Victor. I guess he was pissed his father got sent away. My parents were so scared they had arranged for us to leave for Paris the next morning.

"How did you get out of the house?"

"There was an escape route down in the basement that led to the outside. My father had it done when he built the house. My parents went over the plan with me so many times just in case. It was the middle of the night when we heard the front window downstairs break. I was in bed with my parents and when my father went to see what happened, the entire first floor was up in flames. In the back of their closet was a hidden panel that was made up of stairs that led down to the basement. My father told me to go and that he and my mother would be right behind me. His last words to me were, 'sweetheart, you know what to do'. I climbed down, grabbed the cell phone that was hanging on the wall, and ran exactly where I was supposed to. Within seconds of me getting out, the house exploded. I hid behind a tree and dialed the only number that was programmed into the phone."

"Which was?"

"My Uncle Aiko Kimura. He was there to pick me up within a matter of minutes." Tears filled her eyes. "He took me straight to his house and stayed with me all night while I cried. The next morning, a man came by and dropped off a manila envelope that contained my new identity, birth certificate, and passport. Inside the envelope was a letter from my grandfather telling me that I needed to go with Aiko and start a new life. That was the day Renee Avery Fuller died, and I became Grace Elizabeth Adams."

"Who is your grandfather?"

"He was the director of the FBI."

"Oh." A surprised expression took over my face. "And is Aiko really your uncle?"

"He was my parent's best friend. They served in the military together. They always told me if anything had ever happened to them, Uncle Aiko would take care of me. That day, we boarded a plane to Japan where we lived, and where I trained for years. My uncle told me the world has a lot of bad people in it, and I needed to learn how to survive and protect myself. He taught me everything he knew. I think he knew that if Ives ever found out I was alive, he'd come after me."

"But if only the bodies of your parents were found—"

"My grandfather made sure the report stated two adults and a child were found. He even had a headstone made with my name and placed it next to my parent's graves."

"Jesus Christ, Grace. When was the last time you saw him?"

"A week before the house fire. Three months after my parent's death, my grandfather was killed in a hit and run accident. There were no witnesses, no evidence, nothing. But I knew Ives was responsible for it. Just after I turned twenty,

my uncle and I moved back to Washington where I gradu-
ated from the police academy and began working for the
WSP. I was promoted to detective two years later."

"How did you end up working for the NYPD?"

"You know, I told you enough. I don't want to talk about
it anymore."

I gave her a hand a gentle squeeze.

"Answer me two questions and two questions only."

"What are they?" Her beautiful green eyes stared into
mine.

"Why did you tell me your real name that day on the
beach?"

"I trusted you. Even though I had been taught not to trust
anyone, my heart told me I could trust you. And I wanted to
be me, Renee, even just for a day. With you, I could be her."

"When did you realize it was me? The same boy you met
on the beach all those years ago?"

"By your eyes. I knew it the moment I turned around in
that warehouse and saw you. And also, when you told me
your name was Simon." She smiled. "It was then I knew you
were the boy who I trusted enough to be my real self with
thirteen years ago."

CHAPTER 12

*G*race

He brought his hand up and cradled my chin as his thumb gently swept across my lips. My heart was racing, and I became heated even as a light wind swept over us. Leaning in, he brushed his lips against mine for a soft kiss. I returned it and quickly pulled away.

"We shouldn't." I placed my hand on his chest.

"You're right. I'm sorry. It's just I got swept up—"

"No. Don't apologize. It was nice, but not a good idea."

"Yeah. I get it. I'm going to head inside," he said as he stood up.

"I'll go with you."

He held out his hand and helped me up.

"By the way, Sam is having everyone over tonight to show us the ultrasound pictures. He invited you too."

"I don't know, Simon. That's your family."

"You've already met everyone except Julia, and I'd really like you to meet her. Besides, we're fun and after the past couple of days you've had, I think you could use some fun." His lips gave way to a smirk.

We entered the house and he walked over and opened the refrigerator.

"I wasn't planning on staying."

"Where are you going?" he asked as he turned around.

"I'll get a room somewhere. The last thing I want to do is involve you in this. I never should have called you last night."

"Bullshit." He pointed his finger at me. "I'm already involved and became even more involved when Victor's man shot me. There's one thing you're going to know about me. I don't give up until justice is served. I'm still going after Victor and his crew with or without you. So, we might as well work together. And—you are staying here. You're also coming with me to Sam and Julia's."

"I don't like people telling me what I'm doing." I cocked my head and folded my arms.

"Too bad. Like I said, we're fun people and you need some fun."

I couldn't help how the corners of my mouth forcefully curved themselves upward.

"How's the shoulder."

"It still kind of hurts."

"You wouldn't tell me even if it felt good, would you?" I smirked.

"No. I wouldn't." He gave me a wink and a smile before he walked away.

I let out a deep breath and went upstairs to my room. Pulling my gun from the drawer, I made sure it was loaded and strapped it on me. Grabbing my purse, I walked downstairs and headed for the front door.

"Where are you going?"

"To find your CI. I have a couple questions for him."

"Shit. I'm coming with you."

"It's probably best you don't."

"Are you kidding? I'm not going to have you put him in the hospital with the rest of them."

"Fine. But I can't make any promises."

I opened the door and walked out.

~

"He's running! Why is he running?" I asked Simon as we chased after Vinnie.

"Vinnie, come on," Simon shouted. "We just want to talk."

"No way, Simon. I'm not talking to her. You keep her the hell away from me."

"You're hurting my feelings, Vinnie."

"Good. I don't like you anyway." He tripped and fell to the ground.

As he went to get up, I pushed him, and he fell flat. Pressing my knee as hard as I could into his back, I held him down.

"I thought we were friends," I said to him.

"Simon, help me, man. Come on. She's hurting me."

"You shouldn't have ran, Vinnie. Now you pissed her off."

"If I let go of you, are you going to try and run?"

"No. Please, just get off me."

I stood and tried to help him up, but he pushed my hand away.

"Damn." He frowned. "I don't need your help getting up."

"Who ordered the hit on me?"

"If you know, Vinnie, you better tell her. I can't help you if you don't."

"Tommy ordered it."

"Tommy Cochran? Victor's right-hand man?"

"You know him?" Simon glanced over at me.

"Yeah. I know him."

"When he heard about Cody, he asked me if I knew who did it."

"And you described me to him." I shook my head.

"Yeah. Look, it's nothing personal." He put his hands up. "I didn't know you were a cop. In my defense, you never mentioned that. She never mentioned it, Simon."

"He's right. I didn't. Was Victor the one who told Tommy to send those guys after me?"

"Probably. Tommy doesn't do anything unless Victor tells him to. There's something else I just found out. A big shipment is coming into the port in a couple of days."

"Shipment of what?" Simon asked.

"Military weapons, guns, and drugs. A lot of drugs. Rumor has it that Victor is going to be there because it's his biggest shipment yet and he wants to make sure it goes smoothly."

"What day and time?" I asked.

"I don't know yet. But when I find out, I'll let you know."

"You better, Vinnie. Because if you don't, I can't be responsible for what she might do to you."

"Yeah, yeah. I know."

"Thanks, Vinnie." I gave him a smile. "Next time, don't run."

Simon and I headed back to the car, and when we climbed in, he fastened his seat belt and looked over at me.

"You need to take this car back to the rental shop and get something else. Especially now that they know what you're driving."

"I already thought of that, and I have one waiting for me. That's why I insisted I drive."

"Smart girl." The corners of his mouth curved upward. "I still want to know how you disabled my alarm system."

"A woman never reveals her secrets." I grinned.

CHAPTER 13

Simon

"Hey, bro." I walked into Sam's house and gave him a hug. "Julia, this is Grace. Grace, meet my sister-in-law, Julia."

"It's nice to meet you, Julia." Grace smiled as she extended her hand. "Thank you for inviting me."

"It's nice to meet you too, Grace. Any friend of Simon's is a friend of ours. Can I get you a glass of wine?"

"That would be great. Thank you."

"How's the shoulder?" Sam hooked his arm around me.

"It's okay." I glanced over at Grace who was a few feet away talking to Julia. "It's the best it's felt in a month. Don't tell Grace I said that. After what she put me through, I'm going to let her think otherwise."

Sam let out a chuckle.

"Where is everyone?"

Just as I said that Sebastian and Emilia walked in.

"Hey, bro." Sebastian fisted-bumped me. "You okay?"

"I'm good."

Sam grabbed three beers from the refrigerator, and we stepped onto the patio.

"Where's Stefan?" I asked.

"He said Alex is just finishing up feeding Henry and they'll be right over."

"And Dad?" Sebastian asked.

"I'm sure he'll be here soon."

The sliding door opened, and I heard my mother's voice.

"There you are." She wrapped her arms around my neck from behind and kissed the top of my head. "How is my baby boy doing?"

"I'm fine, Mom."

"I just met Grace when I walked in. She's beautiful, Simon. Is there something you aren't telling me?"

"No, Mom. She's a detective from New York and she's here to help with a case I'm working on."

"But you're not working right now. You're on leave."

"Hey, fam." Stefan stepped onto the patio. "Mom, Lily is looking for you."

"Okay, Stefan. You better still be taking it easy," she said to me.

"I am, Mom. Don't worry."

"Was Lily really asking for her?" Sebastian asked.

"No." Stefan chuckled. "But I figured our brother needed rescuing." He took the seat next to me and grabbed a beer bottle from the table.

"So?" Stefan asked as he looked at Sam. "How was the ultrasound?"

"It was—" he paused.

"Sam?" I cocked my head.

"Julia didn't want me to say anything yet because she wants to tell everyone together, but I can't wait. I need to tell you three right now because I'm—"

"It's twins, isn't it?" Stefan asked.

"Yes. Julia and I are having twins."

Stefan let out a roaring laugh.

"Shut the fuck up, bro! You can't let Julia know you know."

"Wow," I spoke. "Twins, eh? Congrats, bro. I think that's awesome. Stop it." I reached over and slapped Stefan's arm with the back of my hand as he wouldn't stop laughing.

"Two more babies in the family. Congratulations." Sebastian smiled.

"Um, make those three babies. Don't forget about our sibling that's on the way," Stefan said.

"Damn." I shook my head. "How are you feeling about it, Sam?"

"I'm over the moon and happy. But in all honesty, I'm scared shitless. I mean, two babies at the same time?" Sam said.

"Oh, double the mess!" Stefan laughed and Sam shot him a dirty look. "Sorry. It's amazing and you will get through it. Don't forget Mom had four of us at one time. Two will be a piece of cake." He chuckled. "Plus, you have Simon and Sebastian to help you out."

"Uh, and what about you?" Sebastian cocked his head.

"I have two of my own. I already have my hands full."

"So, how's it going with Grace?" Sam asked.

I let out a sigh. "It's going. Listen, there's something I need to talk to you guys about after everyone leaves."

"Sure, bro. We'll stick around," Sebastian said.

"Hello, my four sons." Our father stepped onto the patio and placed his hand on my good shoulder. "How are you, Simon?"

"I'm good, Dad."

"I met Grace this morning. Lovely girl. She's staying with you?"

"Just temporarily. We're working on a case together."

"So she said. Why is she staying with you and not in a hotel?"

"She was and there was a mishap in her room, so I told her to come stay at my place."

"What kind of mishap?"

"Two guys came after her and she beat their asses." Stefan laughed, and I shot him a look.

"Son, is that true?"

"Dad, don't worry about it."

"And what did Stefan mean by 'she beat their asses?'"

"She's highly trained in martial arts. She almost killed the guy who shot me yesterday. He's in pretty bad shape at Cedars."

"Well then, I love that woman already. Make sure to keep her around."

"She lives in New York. Once we catch the guy we're after, she'll be going back home."

"Sam, my parents are here," Julia said as she opened the sliding door.

Sam got up from his seat and went inside.

"Um, bro?" Stefan said as he glanced over. "Jenni is talking to Grace."

"Shit. I forgot that she would be here. It's fine." I furrowed my brows. "Right?"

Sebastian and Stefan both started laughing.

CHAPTER 14

*G*race

Hi, Grace." Lily smiled as she walked over to me.

"Hi, Lily. How are you?"

"I'm good. I like your shoes."

"Thank you." I grinned.

"Hey, kiddo." A beautiful woman walked over with a bright smile. "Hi, I'm Jenni." She extended her hand.

"Grace. It's nice to meet you." I lightly shook her hand.

"Grace had a sleepover at Uncle Simon's last night," Lily said."

"Is that so?" She cocked her head at me.

"Wow. Okay, little miss sunshine, come outside with us." Sam scooped her up.

"Oh my God. It's not what you think." I put my hand up. "He let me stay in his guestroom last night after two guys tried to kill me in my motel room."

"Say what?" She hooked her arm around me and led me away from everyone who was gathered in the kitchen. "Tell me more."

"It was nothing. The guy I'm after sent his men after me."

"Is that how you got that cut?" She pointed to my forehead.

"Yeah."

"Oh my God. You poor girl. They could have killed you. So, Simon is protecting you?"

I couldn't help but laugh. "No. He's not protecting me. We're both after the same guy. Listen, if this is weird for you, I'll go get a hotel room."

"Weird for me? Why would you say that?"

"Well, Lily told me that you sleep over Simon's a lot."

"Out of the mouths of babes." She sighed. "Simon is my best guy friend. That's it. Nothing else. You stay there as long as you need to. Where are you from?"

"New York. I'm a detective with the NYPD."

"Oh. Okay. Now it makes sense."

"Hey, Jenni," Simon spoke as he walked over to us in a nervous manner.

"Hey, friend." She reached up and kissed his cheek. "Grace and I are just talking."

"About?"

"Wouldn't you love to know." A smirk crossed her mouth. "Anyway, we'll chat later, Grace. It was great to meet you."

"You too, Jenni." I smiled.

As soon as she walked away, Simon looked at me.

"You two sleep together, don't you?" My brow arched.

"We used to. It's complicated and a story for later."

"She seems great."

"She is. She's a good friend. Julia said the food is ready, so let's go eat."

As I sat next to Simon and ate, I looked around at his big family. Everyone was eating, laughing, and having a great time. Simon was right. His family was fun, and they were great people.

It had always been just my parents and me. They'd had

me a little later in life, and I was enough for them. After they were murdered, it was just my Uncle Aiko and me, along with some of his family in Japan. I'd learned their culture and their ways, and even though they welcomed me with open arms, I still felt like an outsider.

"Can we have everyone's attention." Julia tapped on a glass. "As you all know, Sam and I had our first ultrasound today. If you'd follow us into the living room, we would love to show you a video that the doctor gave us of the ultrasound."

Everyone got up from their seats and went into the living room. Sam popped in the disc and the images of the ultrasound appeared. I stared at it closely and glanced over at Simon who smiled and gave me a wink.

"This is Baby A, and this little peanut is Baby B." Julie beamed with excitement.

"Twins?" Henry cocked his head at Sam.

"Yeah, Dad. We're having twins." He smiled.

Everyone screamed with excitement and congratulated them both.

"Do you know the sex yet?" Simon's mother asked.

"No. The results are sealed away in an envelope upstairs."

"Which you are to give me right now," Jenni said. "I'll be sending out the invites for the gender, or in this case, genders reveal party in a couple of days."

"Hey, Dad? Do you know what you and Celeste are having yet?" Simon asked.

"We'll find out in a couple of days, son."

"Perfect." Julia smiled. "We can have a joint gender reveal party."

"Thank you, Julia. That sounds like fun, but it's okay."

"No. We're having one for you and Celeste too, Dad. How fun is it going to be to find out at the same time." She grinned.

~

*S*imon
Everyone had left except me and my brothers. Julia was exhausted so she headed up to bed, and Grace went back to my house to call her uncle. Sam grabbed some more beers from the fridge, and we all met outside.

"What did you want to talk to us about?" Sam asked.

"I've met Grace before."

"What?" Sebastian's brows furrowed. "When?"

"When we were both thirteen. Do you remember that time when you and Stefan were really sick, Sam went to work with Dad, and I went to the beach to surf all day? It was about six months after Drew was killed?"

"I remember," Stefan said. "That was the only time we both felt like we were actually dying."

"I was in the water, and she stole my wave. I said something to her about it and she basically ignored me. So, I followed her on to the beach and told her she needed to apologize. Anyway, we ended up talking and spending the rest of the day together surfing and hanging out on the beach."

"Why didn't you ever tell us this?" Sam asked.

"I don't know." I sighed. "I was never going to see her again, so what difference did it make. She was there with her uncle. They were in town for a funeral."

"And you didn't remember her when you saw her in the warehouse?" Stefan asked.

"No, because when I met her all those years ago, her name was Renee, not Grace."

"So, she lied to you and gave you a fake name?" Sebastian asked.

"The opposite. Fuck. It's such a complicated story and it

stays right here. I need all three of you to promise me. You can't even tell the girls."

"Sure, bro. We won't," Sam said as he furrowed his brows. "You know you can trust us."

"Yeah. We have your back. Don't worry," Sebastian said.

I told my brothers everything Grace had told me.

"Damn." Sam shook his head. "That poor girl. She's been through a lot in her life."

"Yeah." I can't even imagine," Sebastian said.

"So, she's like a ninja girl." Stefan grinned. "Or a trained assassin?"

"I guess. I haven't seen her fight, but when I walked into that warehouse and saw Cody on the ground, I was like damn. You saw the pictures of the two guys lying on the floor of her motel room."

"Don't take this the wrong way, brother, but that's really hot." Sebastian smiled.

"You don't have to tell me. I kissed her earlier down at the beach."

"Way to go, bro." Stefan grinned. "Just kissed?"

"She pulled away and said we shouldn't."

"Did you tell her yes you should?" Stefan asked.

"No, bro." I chuckled. "I told her she was right."

"Shit, Simon." Sebastian shook his head. "How are you going to restrain yourself?"

"I don't have a choice. I would give anything to fuck her, but I know boundaries."

"I still can't get over the fact that you two met all those years ago, spent the day together, and you didn't tell us," Sam said. "What other secrets are you keeping from us?"

"Nothing. It wasn't important at the time. I didn't know we'd see each other again twenty years later. It's crazy."

"So, hold on a second," Stefan said. "She surfs?"

"Uh, yeah. You should have seen her twenty years ago.

She would have blown all four of us out of the water back then. I'd hate to see how good she is now. Shit. She'd put us to shame."

"Invite her to surf with us," Sam said.

"I don't know. You know I haven't been able to surf since before the shooting."

"She performed some mojo shit on you earlier. Did it work?" Sebastian asked.

"It does feel better, and I haven't had to take any pain pills. I have physical therapy tomorrow, so we'll see what happens. Maybe by the weekend I'll be able to take the surfboard out."

"Here's to hope." Sam held up his beer and the four of us clanked our bottles against it.

CHAPTER 15

*G*race

    I had just ended my Facetime chat with my uncle when Simon walked in.

"Hey." He smiled. "Did you talk to your uncle?"

"Yeah. I just hung up with him. He's doing good." My lips formed a small smile.

"That's great. I'm sure he misses you."

"Yeah. He does. I really like your family, and I had a wonderful time tonight."

"See." A wide grin crossed his face. "I told you we were great and fun people."

"Yes. You did." I laughed. "So, what's the deal with you and Jenni?"

"We're friends and nothing more. We're not sleeping together. I mean—we did sleep together, but just as friends."

"I'm surprised."

"Why?"

"She's a beautiful woman and she has a great personality. She's totally girlfriend material."

"I agree. And yes, she is totally girlfriend material for a man who's seeking a girlfriend."

I arched my brow. "You're not that man?"

"No." He chuckled. "And if you ask her, she'll tell you the same thing. What we have is pure friendship and nothing else. Besides, I'm a non-committal man."

"Okay Mr. Non-committal man, I'm heading to bed." I smirked as I turned and walked out of the kitchen.

"By the way, I'm still mad at you for what you did to me earlier," Simon shouted as I was halfway upstairs.

"Are you always this dramatic?" I stopped on the stairs and looked at him from over the rail.

The corners of his mouth curved upward, and I just shook my head with a smile and went to my room.

～

*I*t was six a.m. when I walked into Simon's bedroom. The room was dark with a light breeze that gently blew the sheers from the open window.

"Simon." I gently tapped his shoulder. "Simon."

I'd startled him as he reached under his pillow and pulled his gun on me.

"Jesus!" I jumped back.

"Grace?" He lowered his gun. "What are you doing?"

"What are you doing?" I cocked my head at him.

"I could have shot you. Why are you sneaking in my room so early?"

"I wasn't sneaking. I wanted to ask if I could borrow your surfboard."

"Yeah. Sure. You don't have to ask."

"Thanks. Now put that damn gun away." I walked out of his room.

I opened the sliding door, grabbed his surfboard and took

it down to the water. It had been a while since I'd surfed, and I was craving it. I stood at the shoreline and took note of the choppy water. The ocean was angry, and the wind was whipping this morning which was going to make for a more challenging surf. Some would call it dangerous conditions. But for me, it was what I needed.

Putting the board into the water, I climbed on and paddled out. The dream I'd had last night shook me, just like it always did, and I counted on the waves to soothe the pain I'd felt. The waves came at me with a vengeance, but I stood my ground against them for I wasn't about to let them win. I dared them to keep coming, and I rode them as if my life depended on it. After a few waves, I sat on my board and my heart beat out of my chest while exhilaration flowed through me.

~

*S*imon
    I climbed out of bed after she'd walked out of my room and looked out the window. It wasn't a good morning to surf. My phone pinged, so I grabbed it off the nightstand and saw a message in our group chat.

"Bro, what is Grace doing? It's not favorable conditions to be surfing," Sam said.

"I'm going down there now."

Pulling on a pair of sweatpants and a sweatshirt, I slipped on some shoes and headed down to the beach. Standing a few feet from the shoreline, I watched her take on the violent waves.

"Is she crazy?" Sebastian asked as he walked over.

"I think so but she's handling it."

"She's good. Where did she learn to surf like that?"

"I don't know. She woke me up this morning to ask if she could borrow my board, and I pulled a gun on her."

"What the fuck, Simon?"

"She startled me out of a sound sleep."

"You didn't notice it was her before you reached in your nightstand and pulled it out?"

"It was under my pillow."

His brows furrowed at me.

"Why are you keeping it under your pillow?"

"Ever since the shooting—"

"Have you gone to see the psychologist yet?"

"No. I have an appointment next week."

"Good." He patted my back. "I know how strong you are, but when something like that happens, it can fuck with you. I'm going back up to the house. I'll talk to you later."

"See ya, bro."

I stood there and cocked my head at Grace as she grabbed the board and walked out of the water.

"Are you crazy?" I asked.

"Not as crazy as you are for pulling a gun on me earlier." She smirked.

"Sorry about that. You could have gotten hurt out there."

"Nah, you just have to know how to talk to the waves."

I furrowed my brows at her as we stepped inside the house.

"I'm going to take a shower. Can you brew me a cup of coffee?" she asked with a beautiful smile.

"Sure."

"Thanks. I'm sorry for just coming in your room like that." Her eyes stared into mine.

I raised my hand and brought my finger up to the corner of her bandage that was slightly sticking up and gently pressed it down.

"You can come into my bedroom anytime you want." I ran my finger down her cheek.

"You're smooth, detective." The corners of her mouth slightly curved upward.

"I try. Anyway, go take your shower and I'll make you a cup of coffee."

She bit down on her bottom lip before breaking our gaze and heading upstairs.

I let out a sigh as I walked over to the cabinet and took down a cup. When the coffee was done, I took it upstairs and when I went to set it on the dresser, I noticed a picture of her and some guy lying on the bed. It was a close picture, and I noticed the diamond wedding ring on her finger as her hand was planted on his chest. I inhaled a sharp breath and set it back down on the bed when I heard the shower turn off.

CHAPTER 16

*G*race

    Even a hot shower couldn't wash away the feeling of his touch. I trembled when his finger reached up over my wound. Even though he'd gently pushed the corner of the bandage down, I still felt the heat from his finger. My body had craved a man's touch and somehow, I knew he would satisfy everything my body needed. Our short kiss yesterday left me wanting more, but it wasn't a good idea, so I stopped him. Then I watched him last night. His laughter, his strength, the bond he had with his family, and his sexy looks, ignited a fire inside me that wouldn't extinguish. I needed him physically and that was okay because I trusted him.

Securing the towel around my body, I slowly walked down the hall to his bedroom. As I stood in the doorway, I heard the shower turn off in his bathroom. So, I waited. The bathroom door opened, and he walked out in just a towel wrapped around his waist. He stopped and as our eyes locked onto each other's, my mouth gave way to a small smile. He held out his hand, and I walked over to where he stood and took hold of it. Bringing his other hand up, he placed it on the side of my face and brushed his lips against mine.

"Are you sure?" he asked as he broke our kiss.

"Yes." I brought my finger up and wiped the drop of water that sat upon his forehead.

He lifted me up and gently laid me down on the bed. His lips brushed mine as his hands unfastened my towel.

"You are so beautiful." His mouth traveled across my neck and down to my breasts. The feel of his lips wrapped around my hardened peaks sent intense vibrations down below. I let out a soft moan as he placed the palm of his hand against me and dipped his finger inside. It didn't take long for him to bring me to an orgasm as I belted out a pleasurable moan.

"Oh my God," I spoke with bated breath.

"I'm not finished yet." A sexy smirk fell upon his lips as he stroked my torso with his tongue until he reached my throbbing area. His mouth explored me like no other as his hands spread my legs even further. The intensity was overwhelming, and euphoria was mine for the taking. When he was finished, he made his way back up to my lips and kissed me passionately. I wasn't sure how, but his towel was still wrapped around him. The only thing on my mind now was seeing what he had to offer, and what I was in for. Reaching down, I unwrapped the towel and tossed it on the floor.

"I need to grab a condom," he said as he climbed off me.

"Thank you. Thank you. Thank you." I silently thanked the lord for blessing him with a perfectly large package.

He sat on the edge of the bed and took a condom from the drawer of his nightstand.

"Wait, before you put that on."

I climbed off the bed, got down on my knees in front of him, and took his large hard cock in my mouth. I could feel his body tremble as a loud groan erupted in his chest.

"Fuck, Grace. Oh my God," he moaned as his fingers tangled in my hair. "You have to stop because I'm going to come in two seconds. I need to get this damn thing on." He ripped open the package and slipped it over his cock. "Get up here." He grabbed me and pulled me on top of him.

Straddling his muscular body, I slowly lowered myself onto him as we both gasped with pleasure. After riding him for a while, he threw me on my back and thrust in and out of me like a wild beast. My nails dug into the flesh of his back as several moans escaped my lips, and another orgasm took over me. His eyes stared into mine as we both came together in sync, letting each other know the pure pleasure we'd felt.

His body collapsed on mine as we lay there trying to regain our breath. Rolling off me, he removed the condom and threw it in the small trashcan next to his side of the bed. While he lay flat on his back with his hand over his heart, I rolled on my side and ran my finger over his chest.

"How's the shoulder?"

"It's great. Really great." He smiled. "I suppose you want a key now." He smirked.

"Nah. Keep your key. I don't need one to get in." I grinned.

He chuckled. "I don't doubt that."

"I need to find Tommy Cochran."

"Not a good idea. We need to lay low until we find out some more information from Vinnie."

"You really trust that little snake?" I asked.

"He's been my CI since the beginning."

"Why? What do you have on him?"

"Drug possession and illegal firearms charge. He was looking at a hefty prison sentence. We struck a deal, and he knows he has no choice or else he's going away. He won't compromise that because of his four-year-old son. Let me

77

ask you something. Where did you learn to do what you did for me yesterday?"

"My uncle. My body went through a lot during my training period."

"What exactly does your uncle do? I know he was in the military."

"He was counterintelligence for the FBI. He resigned the day after my parents were killed. He told them that it was too much for him to continue working there after what happened and he was going home to Japan. But I know he did it to take care of me."

"And what does he do now?"

"He owns and runs a security firm in Washington."

"Interesting."

"You never answered my question from yesterday." I stroked his chest.

"Which question was that?"

"Was Drew's killer ever found?"

"No. Not yet. I'm working on it still."

"Maybe I can help."

"I appreciate that, but I think we need to focus on Ives right now."

CHAPTER 17

*S*imon
    I couldn't stop thinking about the picture I saw on Grace's bed. The two of them and her ring. It was none of my business, but I wanted to know. Sex with her was incredible and I wanted to know more about her. Normally, I didn't care. But with her, I did. I reached over and softly stroked her cheek with the back of my hand as I stared at her.

"You're so beautiful. You can't lay there and tell me someone hasn't stolen your heart back in New York."

"Nope. Nobody. I'm a non-committal girl." She smirked.

"Is that so?" My brow arched.

"Yeah. Does that surprise you?"

"I don't know."

She lied to me. Perhaps she's divorced. Maybe he broke her heart and trust is an issue as far as relationships are concerned. Who the hell knew? But I was going to find out one way or another.

"Oh shit. What time is it?" I grabbed my phone from the nightstand. "Fuck!"

"What's wrong?"

SANDI LYNN

"I missed my physical therapy appointment."

"Can you call and see if they can let you come anyway?"

"No. They have strict scheduling. Someone distracted me." The corners of my mouth curved upward.

"I'm sorry." She chewed her bottom lip.

"Nah. Don't ever apologize for that." I rolled on top of her and brushed my lips against hers.

After I finished getting dressed, I grabbed my phone, went downstairs, and sent a message to my brothers in our group chat.

"I need to talk. Sebastian, where are you today?"

"Emilia's. What's wrong?"

"Sam and Stefan. Can you meet me at Emilia's for lunch?"

"I can be there in about thirty minutes," Sam said.

"I'm wrapping up at a job right now, but I can be there in about thirty minutes as well. You okay?" Stefan asked.

"I'm fine. I'll see you there."

"I'll make sure lunch is ready when you get here," Sebastian said.

"Hey, what are you doing?" Grace smiled when she walked in.

"I'm actually leaving to go and meet my brothers for lunch."

"It seems like you hang out with your brothers a lot."

"Just about every day."

"That's really nice. Never take your family for granted, Simon. Just don't." She looked down.

"Hey." I placed my finger under her chin and lifted it, so her eyes met mine. "I don't, and I never will. I'm sorry about your parents, Grace."

"Thanks, but I'm good. Really, I am. It's just sometimes I wonder how different my life would be if they were still alive. If—you know what? Go meet your brothers. I'm heading out."

80

"Where are you going?"

"Just to run a few errands."

"Okay. I'll see you when I get back." I leaned in and brushed my lips against hers.

~

"*H*ey, Simon." Ashley smiled when I stepped through the door of Emilia's.

"Hey, Ash. Are my other brothers here yet?"

"Not yet. I'll go tell Sebastian you're here."

"No need. I'll go find him myself. Kitchen?"

"Yeah."

I walked back to the kitchen and saw my brother and Emilia locked in a kiss.

"If the two of you want to screw in the office, I'll cover the kitchen for you." I smiled.

"Shut up." Sebastian laughed.

"Hi, Emilia."

"Hey, Simon. I'm on my way out. Your brother made me lunch."

"Isn't that sweet of him." I placed my hand over my heart. "Wouldn't it have been even sweeter if he personally delivered it to you?"

"Now that you mention it." Emilia's brows furrowed at my brother.

"I can't leave, douchebag." He threw a towel at me. "It's peak lunchtime, and I'm short-staffed."

"I'm going to the table. I'll see you out there. Bye, Emilia."

"Bye, Simon. By the way, I really like Grace."

"Yeah. She's a great woman." I smiled.

Just as I was walking out of the kitchen, Sam was walking in.

"There you are," he said. "Stefan is on his way. Let's go sit down."

We sat at our family table and Courtney, our waitress, walked over with four single malt scotches.

"Sebastian said to send these over to you boys."

"Thanks, Courtney."

"Thanks." I smiled.

I picked up my glass and as I took a drink, Stefan sat down next to me.

"Damn. Traffic is a bitch today." He picked up his glass of scotch.

Sebastian walked over and set our plates down in front of us. He never bothered asking what we wanted. He just always knew.

"So, what's going on?" Sam asked.

"Earlier, I made Grace a cup of coffee while she was in the shower and when I took it up to her room, there was picture lying on her bed."

"Of?" Stefan asked.

"Her and some guy."

"Who was he?" Sebastian asked.

"I'm going to assume her husband since she was wearing a wedding ring."

"What?" Sam's brows furrowed.

"She's married, bro?" Stefan asked.

"Well, she isn't wearing a ring and she told me today that she's a non-committal type of girl."

"Why would she tell you that?" Sam asked.

I took in a deep breath.

"We had sex." I brought my glass up to my lips.

"Shit, bro. You move fast." Stefan smirked. "Just yesterday she told you a kiss wasn't a good idea. She didn't hurt you, did she?" He let out a laugh.

"Shut the hell up. I tried to fish for information by asking her if anyone has stolen her heart back in New York. That's when she said no and that she's a non-committal girl."

"And that's all she said?" Sebastian asked. "Nothing about the guy you saw in the picture?"

"Nope. But I didn't tell her I saw the picture."

"She's keeping that info from you for a reason," Sam said.

"Maybe something happened, and she doesn't want to talk about it," Stefan spoke.

"Bro, you're the one with the good instincts. What is your gut telling you?" Sebastian asked.

"That's the thing. I'm not sure." My brows furrowed.

CHAPTER 18

*S*imon

After doing some digging around, I found out the name of Grace's partner back in New York. Pulling my phone from my pocket, I dialed her number.

"Detective Carrie Brady."

"This is Detective Simon Kind with the LAPD. I was hoping you could answer some questions about your partner, Grace Adams."

"Grace? Detective Kind, Grace is no longer my partner or with the NYPD. What is this about? Is she in trouble?"

"No. She's not. What do you mean she's no longer with the NYPD?"

"Six months ago, right after her husband was murdered, she walked into the station, handed in her gun and badge and said she quit. No one's heard from her since."

"How was he murdered?" I asked.

"She came home one night and found him shot to death in their bed."

"Jesus. Do they know who did it?"

"No. The place was clean. There were no fingerprints or anything."

"Thank you, Detective Brady. Is there a way you can send me the report?"

"You know I can't do that."

"I understand. Thank you."

"Is she there in Los Angeles?" she asked.

My instincts told me not to tell her.

"She was but she seems to have disappeared."

"It seems she's good at that. If you hear from her, tell her to call me."

"I will."

I ended the call and let out a sigh. If I were Grace, I would have taken a copy of that report and kept it. Getting up from behind my desk, I went into her room and dug through the bag she had sitting on the chair. Suddenly, I heard the front door open downstairs, so I quickly put everything back in her bag and went into the bathroom and shut the door. I could hear her coming up the stairs, so I flushed the toilet and stepped out of the bathroom.

"Hey." She smiled.

"You're back. Did you get what you needed?"

"Yeah. I did." She held up two bags.

"Good." I gave her a small smile and headed downstairs.

An anger stirred inside me as I placed my hands on the granite countertop of the island. She was still lying to me, and I wasn't putting up with it. I needed to confront her, and I didn't know how she was going to react.

"What's wrong?" she asked when she walked into the kitchen.

"Why didn't you tell me you no longer work for the NYPD?" I slowly glanced up at her.

"What?" There was a nervousness in her voice. "Why do you think that?"

"I called your partner, Detective Carrie Brady."

"You what? How dare you!" she shouted.

"No!" I angrily pointed my finger at her. "How dare you fucking lie to me, Grace! You didn't tell me that or about your husband's murder!" I shouted back.

She took in a sharp breath as tears filled her eyes.

"You had no right." She shook her head.

"I found the picture of the two of you. Why didn't you tell me?"

"You went through my things?" Her teary eyes narrowed.

"No. I went to set the cup of coffee I made you this morning on the dresser for when you got out of the shower, and I saw it lying on the bed. I gave you a chance to tell me earlier, but you told me you're a non-committal girl. Which obviously is another lie. So, you left me no choice, Grace. I needed to find out on my own. Now, you can either tell me or get the hell out of my house."

"Fine. I'll go." She turned and ran up the stairs.

Shit.

I ran up after her and when I entered her room, she was zipping up her bag.

"Just stop it, Grace!" I shouted.

"Stop what, Simon?" She turned around and looked at me. "You told me to get the hell out of your house, so I am."

"I gave you a choice. You said you trusted me."

She lowered her head and then threw her bag on the bed.

"You want the truth?" she shouted in anger. "They killed him because of me, and I will never forgive myself for that."

I stood there in shock for a moment and then I walked over to where she stood, wrapped my arms around her and pulled her into me.

"You can't blame yourself."

"Yes, I can." She broke our embrace and stared into my

eyes. "He didn't deserve that. He was a good man." Tears streamed down her cheeks.

"Do you know who did it?" I asked her as I gently wiped away her tears.

She slowly nodded her head.

"I have a pretty good idea. But I do know Ives was behind it."

"Do you have proof?"

"Actually, I do."

She took a seat on the edge of the bed.

"I went to New York because my uncle and I had found out that Ives had set up a bunch of shell companies there. He was using them to clean money, and I was tracking him. After I had a run in with Tommy Cochran and beat his ass, I arrested him, and he was let go on a 'technicality' which was bullshit. That's when I'd suspected someone in the department was a mole."

"Who?"

"I didn't have a chance to figure that out before I left."

"Your ex-partner said they found no fingerprints or anything in your home. How can you be sure it was Ives?"

When I came home and found my husband lying in a pool of blood in our bed, there was a post it note attached to his forehead."

"What the hell? What did it say?"

"Welcome back from the grave, Renee. Your parents would be so proud."

"Jesus, Grace." I shook my head. "I'm so sorry." I gave her hand a squeeze.

"I took the note for obvious reasons. Then after Connor's funeral, I quit. I knew I wouldn't be able to investigate and handle Ives the way I wanted to, and I knew I was being watched. So, I went back to my uncle's place in Washington, grieved, and then tracked Ives here. That's how I found

Vinnie. But I didn't know he was your CI. I started with him which led me to Cody. Now that Ives figured out I'm here, he's going to stop at nothing to kill me."

"I'm not going to let that happen."

"Cody made a mistake shooting you. Ives tries his best to stay off the radar of the police. The last thing he needs is that kind of attention drawn to him. They killed my parents, my grandfather, and my husband. Now, I'm going to kill every one of them until I get to Ives and kill him myself. That's why I quit the NYPD. I'm no longer playing by their rules."

"You just can't go around the city killing people."

"Don't tell me you wouldn't do the same thing if they killed your family."

I looked away from her and let out a sigh. She had a point.

My phone rang, and when I pulled it from my pocket, I saw Vinnie was calling.

"What's up, Vinnie?" I put him on speaker.

"That shipment is coming in tonight at eleven o'clock. There's something else."

"What?"

"When the shipment arrives, another shipment is going out."

"What kind of shipment?"

"Women who were sold to various buyers. I overhead Tommy talking. They're being kept in a house owned by some guy named Malcolm Ross. That's all I know. I gotta go. Someone is coming."

Click.

"Malcolm Ross is the man who owns Cyber Tech Securities," Grace said. "We were watching him back in New York for various crimes, but he covers his tracks so well, we couldn't get him." She grabbed her phone.

"Who are you calling?"

"My uncle."

CHAPTER 19

*G*race

"Hey. Malcolm Ross is involved with Ives and he's keeping sold women at a house he owns here in Los Angeles. I need an address on him now and a layout of the property."

"Grace, if we go to Malcolm's house and get those women out, it's going to fuck up the shipment tonight. We need to wait."

"We are going to wait. But we're also going to stake out the house and follow them. Actually, I don't want you involved."

"What?" His brows furrowed.

"You're on leave, Simon. You will get in serious trouble. Plus, I can't let anything happen to you."

"You're sweet, Grace. But you're also fucking crazy if you don't think I'm doing this with you. Plus, Roman will back us up. I'll go give him a call now." He stepped out of the room.

*W*e were on the hillside looking through binoculars when we saw two large semi-trucks pull up at Malcolm's house. The four men who were standing guard outside walked to the back of the trucks.

"It looks like they're unloading something," Simon said. "Are those crates?"

"Shit. Call Cody right now!" I yelled.

Simon pulled his phone from his pocket.

"It went straight to voicemail," he said.

"They knew we were going to the port. They must have found out Cody is your CI."

"FUCK!" Simon yelled as he kept trying to call Cody. "I need to call Roman."

Suddenly, I felt something pointed at the back of my head.

"The two of you better not move," I heard a voice from behind.

Simon and I slowly turned our heads and looked at each other. The two men reached down and took our guns from us.

"Get up!" One of them shouted.

We both slowly stood with our hands up.

"Now slowly turn around."

We did as we were instructed while they both pointed their guns at our faces.

"Detective Grace Adams," the large man with the scar across his face spoke. We meet again. Do you remember me?"

"How could I forget? One of the best times of my life was when I smashed your face through a glass table."

"What a pleasure it is going to be killing you. Tommy wanted to do it himself, but he's a little busy right now."

"Nah, he doesn't have a big enough dick to do it himself.

But you," I looked down, "you seem to have one to match your large body, so I have no doubt you're going to try and kill me. 'Try' being the operative word."

He let out a sinister laugh.

"Grace, stop antagonizing him," Simon whispered.

"He can take it. Can't you, big boy." I smirked.

"Such a filthy mouth for a beautiful woman," he said.

I looked over his shoulder and nodded my head. "Hey, Tommy."

When the guys turned their heads, Simon and I both kicked their guns out of their hands and took them down. The big guy punched me and sent me flying across the dirt.

"Grace!" Simon shouted.

The area around me was spinning as I tried to focus. Looking over to my right was a gun. As I reached for it, the big guy pinned my arms down with his heavy boots as he stared down at me.

"Ouch, you asshole."

"You're not as tough as you think you are," he said.

"Weren't you ever taught to secure the legs of the person you're trying to kill first!" I lifted my leg straight up and hit him in the balls as hard as I could. He grabbed them and as he went to fall on me, I rolled out of the way and grabbed the gun.

"Time's up, big guy." I cocked the gun and pointed it down at him. "Like I said earlier, 'try' being the operative word." I pulled the trigger and shot him in the head.

Another gunshot went off and when I turned around, Simon had the other man on the ground.

"Are you okay?" he asked.

"I'm fine. You?"

"Yeah. Good distraction," he said as he wiped the blood from his mouth.

"Thanks." I gave him a light smile.

Suddenly, another vehicle pulled up and Simon and I immediately held up our guns.

"Hold up. It's Roman," he shouted out the driver's side window.

We both lowered our weapons.

Roman got out of the car and ran up to us.

"You two okay?"

"Yeah," Simon said. "How did you know where we were?"

"Your location on your phone is on, remember? We found Vinnie. He's in bad shape, but I think he'll pull through."

"Shit." Simon shook his head.

"We need to get down to that house," I spoke.

"I already called for backup. They'll be here soon."

"Then we better hurry up."

"You're going to need these," Roman said as he handed us two bulletproof vests. "I can't believe you're not wearing one." He looked at Simon.

"I was going to put it on before we made it down to the house."

The windows of the van were heavily tinted so when we pulled up, the men outside wouldn't know any better and think we were the two men who lay dead on the hilltop. When we reached the winding road that led to the house, one of the guards stood in the middle of it and held up his hand forcing us to stop.

"Really?" My brows furrowed.

"I don't think he's going to move," Simon said.

"You sure about that?" I lowered the driver's side window just enough for the barrel of my gun to fit through and fired it twice, hitting him both times in the chest. He went down and I pushed on the gas pedal.

"For the love of God, do not run over him!" Roman shouted.

"I wasn't planning on it." I swerved and missed hitting his body. "Do you think I'm that cruel?"

"I don't know what to think about you yet, Grace," Roman said, and Simon snickered.

CHAPTER 20

*G*race

We parked the van down the road from the house and quietly snuck around the back. We were spotted and the firing began. I'd lost track of Simon and Roman as I quietly stepped inside the house. Two men came at me, and I took care of them as I emptied my clip into their bodies. I didn't have time to reload when two more guys entered the room. I threw my gun down and took them on myself. They both got a few good punches in, but I quickly put them down. Grabbing my gun, I reloaded it.

"It's nice to see you again, Renee."

Looking up, I saw Tommy standing there gripping Simon with a gun pointed to the side of his head.

"Tommy Fucking Cockroach."

"It's Cochran, you bitch!" he shouted. "Put the gun down or your partner gets a bullet put through his pretty little head.

"He's not my partner. I work alone." I pointed my gun at him. "So do what you have to do."

"Jesus Christ, Grace!" Simon said.

"You ruined my plans back in New York."

"Really? And what plan was that?"

"I was going to kill you after I killed your husband. But then you had to go and disappear."

A sick feeling rose in the pit of my stomach.

"Don't you ever talk about my husband."

"Do you want to know what happened that night, Renee?"

"Shut up!" I shouted.

"He was so scared. When he opened his eyes and saw the barrel of my gun staring him in the face, I swear he peed the bed."

I swallowed hard as my heart beat out of my chest.

"He asked me who I was and to be fair, I told him. I have this thing about wanting people to know who I am before I put a bullet in their head."

"Why? Because it's the only way people ever notice a cockroach like you?"

"Shut up!" He cocked his gun.

"Let him go, Tommy. This is between me and you."

"I'm afraid I can't do that. Mr. Ives wants everyone close to you dead. You fuck with his family; he fucks with yours."

I cocked my gun.

"Stupid, stupid girl." Tommy's lips formed a sinister smile.

"Even if I put the gun down, you're still going to shoot me and then shoot him."

"True. It seems you know me all too well, sweetheart."

"See, here's the thing, Tommy. I'm faster than you." I pulled the trigger and shot him right in the center of his forehead and he fell back.

"What the fuck!" Simon shouted.

"You're welcome. Now let's go find Ives."

"You could have missed and shot me, Grace!"

"I could have, but I didn't. Stop being so dramatic,

Simon," I said as we headed up the winding staircase. "You go find the women and I'll take care of Ives."

"I'm not leaving you. Roman is taking care of the women."

"I could get you killed." I glanced over at him.

"That is very true, but I guess I'll have to take my chances."

We approached a set of locked double doors at the end of the hall. Kicking it in, the room was empty but there was a secret wall that was half open.

"Shit," Simon said as we approached it.

We climbed down the tall ladder that led us to a large storage area.

"You go that way, and I'll go this way," I whispered. "Whatever you do, don't shoot him. Promise me."

"I promise. But if he tries to kill me, I'm shooting his ass."

"Fine. Just shoot him somewhere it won't kill him. Please."

He shot me a look and went the opposite way I did.

"Your time is up Ives. Come out now and face me, you fucking ball less coward."

"Such strong words for a scared little girl." He emerged from behind a large wooden crate.

"Really? Out of all the illegal guns in this place and you have to resort to that one?" I cocked the gun I had pointed at him.

"Don't underestimate its power. One shot in that pretty little head of yours and you will be completely unrecognizable. That is why this beauty was created."

"I'll take my chances, Victor."

"Imagine my surprise when I found out you were alive."

"Humor me. How did you find out?"

"After you had your fun with Tommy back in New York, I sent someone to take pictures of you. I wanted to see what the woman looked like who roughed up my right-hand man and arrested him. When I saw the pictures, one resembled the same one that was taken of you when you were a little girl. Same eyes, same look on your face, only older. So, I had my men go to your grave site and dig up your body. Imagine our surprise when the casket was empty. How did you escape that house fire I had the pleasure of setting?"

Simon slowly walked up next to me with his gun pointed at Victor.

"I was trained well by my parents in case of an emergency."

"Too bad your parents didn't make it out in time before it burned. Watching that house explode from across the street was the highlight of my day." He grinned.

I could feel my heart wanting to escape my chest.

"And such a tragedy about your grandfather. Then, there was Connor. You poor thing having to find your husband like that only after three months of marriage."

"Don't listen to him, Grace," Simon said.

"Simon, put your gun away."

"What? No."

"Do it!" I shouted. "I need you to step twenty feet to the right."

"Grace—"

"Just do as I ask! You won, Victor." I showed him my gun as I slowly lowered it and set it on the ground. "You have taken everything I've loved away from me. You took my life away, and I really have nothing to live for anymore." Dropping my hand, I slid the gun across the floor to him. "Except this!" I quickly reached around and pulled the gun I had tucked into the back of my pants and emptied it into Victor.

I froze as I watched his body hit the ground. Simon reached over and placed his hand on mine and slowly lowered it.

"LAPD! Drop your weapon!"

97

Setting the gun down, I put my hands up and slowly turned around.

"Enough. She's working undercover for the FBI," Jonah Turner spoke as he walked in. "Are you okay, Grace."

"I'm fine, Jonah."

"It's over." He gripped my shoulders. "It's finally over."

"This is Detective Simon Kind. Simon, this is Jonah Turner."

"Good work, Detective." He extended his hand to Simon.

"Thank you, sir."

CHAPTER 21

*S*imon
"Kind, you are to be in my office tomorrow morning at nine a.m." my captain spoke in a stern voice as he approached me.

"Yes, sir."

"Calm yourself, James," Jonah Turner said as he placed his hand on his shoulder. "The LAPD gets full credit for this take down. "Grace was never here, and we'll discuss it further in the morning. Do either of you need medical attention?"

"He probably does, but I don't," Grace spoke.

"Why do you think I need medical attention?" I glanced over at her.

"Why are you being dramatic?"

"Why do you always think I'm being dramatic?" I asked her as we walked away.

"Because you are."

The corners of my mouth curved upward as I hooked my arm around her.

"I need an ice pack and some alcohol."

"Me too."

~

e stepped inside the house and went straight to the kitchen. Opening the freezer, I grabbed two ice packs and handed one to Grace.

"We have a lot to talk about," I said as I picked up the bottle of scotch and poured it into two glasses.

The sliding door opened, and Sam and Stefan stepped inside.

"We saw you pull up," Sam said.

"Damn, you two. What the hell happened?"

"We got Ives and his men tonight. It's over," I said as I gripped my shoulder.

"Congratulations, bro," Sam said. "Are you okay?"

"I'm fine."

"And you, Grace?" Sam glanced over at her.

"Just another day of work." The corners of her mouth curved upward as she held the ice pack on her cheek.

"Do you two need anything?" Stefan asked.

"Nah. This is all we need." I held up the bottle of scotch.

"For sure." Sam smirked. "We'll let you two get some rest and we'll talk tomorrow."

My brothers left and I poured Grace another scotch.

"You lied to me, again."

"Ugh. Can we not talk about this now? I'm too tired and sore. I just need to get in a hot bubbly tub."

"Then let's go. We'll talk in the tub."

She sat there at the table and furrowed her brows at me.

"What? A hot bubbly tub sounds nice and relaxing. So, come on." I held out my hand to her.

"Just because we had sex one time—"

"Shut up, Grace, and give me your hand."

She placed her hand in mine and I helped her up from the table. As I started the water for the bath, I glanced over as she pulled off her shirt and looked in the mirror at the large bruise on her side.

After carefully stripping out of my clothes, I climbed in the tub and Grace followed. When she laid back, I flinched.

"Sorry," she said as she shifted her body, so she wasn't leaning against my injured shoulder. "As soon as we get out, I'll rub some oil on it."

"Um—no. It's fine."

She let out a laugh. "I'll be gentle. I promise."

I secured my arms around her and immediately felt her body relax.

"Why didn't you tell me you were undercover for the FBI?"

"I couldn't, and I need you to understand that."

"Were you undercover when you went to New York?"

"No. It wasn't until after Connor was killed and I went back to Washington when Jonah paid us a visit. Ives had left the country. It's what he did. When he felt there was too much heat on him, he fled, but he always came back at some point. When shit started going down here in L.A., Jonah asked for my help because he knew I would stop at nothing to get Ives."

"Does he know who you really are?"

"Yeah. He worked directly under my grandfather, and he was his best friend. But I didn't know that until he paid me a visit. My uncle did, but never told me. After Ives had my grandfather killed, he disappeared for over a decade."

"So now what?" I asked as I softly stroked her arm. "Are you going to work for the FBI?"

"No. I already told Jonah once this was over, I was done. I love being a detective, but I don't want to work for the FBI. I guess I'll take some time off, regroup, and figure things out."

"Are you okay, Grace? Those things both Tommy and Victor said to you about your family and Connor—"

"I'm fine, Simon. Their words gave me even more strength."

"I didn't know you were only married three months. How long were you with him?"

"We dated for about a year when he asked me to marry him. We were in Vegas for his birthday when he proposed. He told me he couldn't wait, and he wanted to get married before we left in one of those little chapels. I told him he was crazy but I loved him and so we did. When we got back to New York, we had a small reception with my uncle, Connor's family, and our friends. His parents blame me for his death."

"How could they?"

"They told me it was because of my job that got him killed and they warned him not to get involved with me. He should have listened."

"Stop, Grace. You can't blame yourself." My grip around her tightened. "Our line of work is dangerous, but we can't shelter ourselves from people because of it."

CHAPTER 22

*G*race

When we climbed out of the tub, Simon grabbed a towel and wrapped it around my body. Bringing my fingers up to his shoulder, I lightly traced around it.

"I'll go get the oil."

"You know what? It feels a lot better now. So much better after that bath."

"Stop being so dramatic." The corners of my mouth curved upward as I walked out of the bathroom.

As I slipped on a pair of pajama bottoms and a tank top, my phone rang, and my uncle was Facetiming me. Sitting on the edge of the bed, I answered it.

"Hey." I smiled.

"My darling Grace. How are you?"

"I'm fine, Uncle Aiko. It's over."

"I know, sweetheart. You did good and I'm very proud of you. Take some time and recenter yourself. Reflect on what has happened and put it behind you."

"I will. I'm just really tired right now."

"I can see that. Get some sleep and we'll talk soon. When are you coming back to Washington?"

"I don't know yet."

"Okay. When you're ready, you'll know. I love you, Grace."

"I love you too, Uncle Aiko."

I ended the call, grabbed the bottle of oil, and walked into Simon's room.

"We're you talking to someone?"

"My uncle just called to find out how I'm doing."

"I'd love to meet him one day."

"I think you'd like him." I smiled. "Now, sit your ass down on the bed."

He let out a sigh and took a seat.

"You better be gentle. I'm already sore enough as it is."

After I rubbed the oil into his shoulder, I went into the bathroom and washed my hands.

"I'm going to head to bed," I said.

"Sleep in my bed tonight."

"Simon, I—"

"You shouldn't be alone after everything you've been through tonight."

He walked over and pulled the covers back.

"Come on. Climb in. I promise I'll behave myself." He smirked.

A small smile crossed my lips as I climbed in, and he pulled the covers over me. Walking over to his side, he climbed in and held his arm out, signaling me to snuggle my body against his.

"Did you set the alarm for tomorrow morning?" I asked.

"Unfortunately." He let out a sigh. "I'm sure my ass is toast. I'm probably looking at a hefty suspension."

"I doubt it. Jonah will talk to your captain."

"Somehow, I don't think my captain will care. I've broken

more rules in my career as a detective than he's ever seen, and he's tired of it."

I let out a soft laugh as my head lay on his chest.

"Go to sleep, detective."

He pressed his lips against the top of my head as I slowly closed my tired eyes.

When the alarm went off the following morning, I was rolled on my side with Simon's arm hooked securely around me. I let out a moan as my body ached from head to toe. Rolling over, he shut off his alarm and then snuggled up against me, pressing his lips on my shoulder.

"Good morning," he whispered.

"Good morning." I rolled over and faced him.

"How do you feel?" he asked.

"Sore. You?"

"Same. I need to get up and get dressed."

"I'm coming with you."

"I'm not sure that's a good idea."

"You know, it's way too early to argue with me."

"Fine. We can argue about it later." He kissed my forehead and climbed out of bed.

"I'll go make us some coffee."

I went downstairs to the kitchen and popped a k-cup in the Keurig. When I heard a light knock on the sliding door, I looked over and saw Sebastian standing there.

"Good morning." I opened the door.

"Morning. I know it's early. Simon is usually up by now," he said as he stepped inside the kitchen.

"He is. He's in the shower."

"Ouch." He pointed to the bruise on my cheek. "Are you okay?"

"I'm fine. You should see the other guy. Oh wait, you can't. He's dead."

"Oh." He chuckled. "Anyway, I just wanted to drop off

these muffins from the restaurant. They're Simon's favorite." He handed me a white box and I lifted the lid to peek inside.

"Oh wow. These look delicious. Did you make them?"

"No. My pastry chef did. She's amazing."

"Hey, brother." Simon walked into the kitchen in a pair of sweatpants. "I thought I heard you." He gave him a light hug.

"You look pretty banged up, bro. You okay?"

"Yeah. I'm good." He smiled. "I'm just getting ready to head to the station. The captain wants to see me after last night."

"Are you in trouble?"

"Most likely. I'm probably going be suspended for a while in addition to my medical leave."

"Don't listen to him. He's being dramatic."

Simon glanced over at me with a narrowed eye. "You really need to stop saying that."

I grabbed my coffee and gave him a smile. "I would if you would stop being dramatic all the time. It was nice to see you, Sebastian."

"You too, Grace."

CHAPTER 23

Simon

"I like her, bro."

"Yeah. She's a great woman. Thanks for the muffins." I took one from the box and bit into it.

"You're welcome. Now that your guy is caught—"

"You mean dead." I smirked.

"Okay. Dead. Is Grace sticking around or is she leaving?"

"I don't know. She hasn't said and I haven't asked."

"I see. I have to run before Emilia leaves for the office. Good luck at the station and let us know what happens."

"I will, brother."

That was the question that had kept me up all night. Was she going to stay or was she going to leave? Either way, I needed to prepare myself.

I ran upstairs to finish getting dressed and then Grace and I headed to the station. When we walked in, all my fellow officers began clapping and patting me on the back.

"Okay, okay. Let's not make a big deal about it." I grinned.

"Kind, in my office!" my captain shouted.

"Here we go." I sighed.

When Grace followed me into his office, my captain didn't look pleased.

"May I ask why you brought her?"

"In case you don't know who I am, my name is Detective Grace Adams, formally of the NYPD." She extended her hand.

"Captain James Burrows." He lightly shook her hand.

"Just to clear something up, Simon didn't have a choice." Her brow raised at him as I stood there holding my breath.

"You must have some higher up connections within the FBI, young lady. I was all set to suspend your dumb ass, Kind. But I was told by the chief not to, even though you broke so many rules. You know I don't like people telling me how to run my department." He pointed his finger at me.

"Yeah, Captain. I know. I'm sorry. It's just—"

"He was helping me. And because of his help and knowledge, we got Ives and his men off the streets and saved many people's lives. Lives the LAPD saved. Am I right, Captain Burrows?"

He stared at her for a moment.

"Right. How do you two know each other?" His brows furrowed.

"We've known each other since we were thirteen years old, right?" Grace glanced over at me with a smile.

"Yes. She's right. I've known this woman for the past twenty years."

"How's the shoulder, Kind?"

"It's a lot better."

"Did you have your appointment yet with the psychologist?"

"That appointment is tomorrow."

"Good. You can report back to work on Monday."

"Really?" I smiled.

"Yes. I know Roman can't wait to have his partner back."

"Thanks, Captain. I appreciate it."

"You're welcome. Now, get out of here. I have a press conference to attend."

~

*S*ebastian
I created a new group chat that included Sam, Stefan, Emilia, Julia, and Alex. I purposely left out Simon because I didn't want him to know about it.

"Can you all meet me at Emilia's at 1:00 pm? We need to have a family meeting."

"Why didn't you include Simon?" Sam asked.

"Because this meeting is about him."

"I'll be there, babe," Emilia responded.

"Me too," Julia said.

"I'll be there," Alex wrote.

"Stefan and I will be there, bro."

"Lunch?" Stefan wrote.

"Yes, bro. Don't worry." I sent the rolling eyes emoji.

I prepped a few different kinds of paninis and salads for when my family arrived.

"Hey, Courtney, get the family table set up. There'll be six of us."

"Got it, boss."

It was five minutes to one and my family had arrived on time. Giving Emilia a kiss, I took the seat next to her.

"What is this about?" Sam asked.

"As you are all aware, the case Simon was working on with Grace is now closed."

"Yeah, I heard it was a bloodbath." Stefan shook his head.

"He and Grace are pretty bruised up. I was over at his house this morning. I asked him if Grace was going to stay or if she was going to leave now that the case is over. He said he didn't know, but I could tell he was worried about it."

"Worried about her staying?" Stefan asked.

"No. I think what our brother is trying to say is that Simon is worried she's going to leave," Sam said.

"Correct. We all like Grace in the very short time we've known her, right?"

"Yeah. Of course," everyone spoke.

"I don't know about you, but I notice the excitement in his eyes when he looks at her, and we all know what that look means."

"I've noticed," Sam said.

"Me too."

"Jenni mentioned it to me the other night," Julia said.

"We need to get Grace to want to stay in California," I spoke. "She doesn't have any family except an uncle in Washington. Simon said she doesn't work for the NYPD anymore, so that means she doesn't have a job and isn't tied to anywhere specific. Em, Julia, and Alex, take her out, have fun and include her in as much as you can. We need to make her feel like she's part of our family. Julia, talk to Jenni and have her do the same. She's really good at that."

"I will."

"I hear what you're saying, Sebastian, but what if she just packs up and decides to leave?" Sam asks.

"We'll have to stop her."

"And if she doesn't feel the same way about Simon?" Alex asked.

"I think she does." Emilia smiled.

"So, we're playing cupid?" Stefan asked.

"Pretty much. Are we all in agreement to try and get Grace to stay?"

"Yes." Everyone nodded and spoke at the same time.

After the girls left, Sam and Stefan stayed back for a moment.

"What's going to happen if this blows up in our face?" Sam asked.

"Yeah. What if Grace wants more from Simon? You know he isn't a willing participant in the relationship department," Stefan spoke.

"Let's pray it doesn't blow up. And if we know and can feel that Simon is in love with her and he's just being a fucking douchebag like we were, then we'll have to deal with him. So, my brothers," I placed my hands on their shoulder, "brace yourself for the storm that might be coming."

CHAPTER 24

*G*race
  Simon and I stayed at the police station for a while, and he introduced me to all his friends and coworkers. I could tell he was very respected and well-liked by his peers.

"Hey, Grace? Can I talk to you for a minute?" Roman asked.

"Sure, Roman."

He led me over to a quiet corner while Simon sat at his desk talking with his people.

"What's up?" I asked.

"You can't mention this to Simon. I'm not ready to tell him yet."

"Okay. You have my word. I won't say anything."

"I'm applying for the FBI, and I need your advice."

"That's great, Roman. You'd make a really good FBI agent. I'm not sure what advice I can give since I'm not one. I only was doing them a favor undercover. But I know someone who can tell you everything you need to do and know, and maybe put in a good word."

"Really? Who?"

"My Uncle Aiko." I pulled out my phone. "Give me your number."

As he rattled it off, I typed it in my phone and then sent him a text message with my uncle's contact information. Then I sent a message to my uncle, who responded immediately.

"There. I sent you his number and he just told me he'd be more than happy to talk with you."

"Wow, Grace. Thank you. Thank you so much."

"You're welcome." I gave him a smile.

"What's going on over here," Simon asked.

"Roman was just asking me about my martial arts training."

"Over here in the corner?" Simon's brow arched.

"It was too noisy over there, partner." Roman placed his hand on Simon's shoulder. "Everyone is happy you're back on Monday and so I am. I cannot wait to have my partner back. I've missed you."

"I've missed you too, man. It'll be good to get back to working together again."

"If you'll excuse me, I have some paperwork to catch up on. Catch you later. Bye, Grace."

"Bye, Roman. He's a nice guy."

"Yeah. He's one of the best partners I've ever had. I love him like a brother. Are you ready to go see Vinnie?"

"Yeah. I hope I don't give him a heart attack." I laughed.

"Just keep your distance, and don't get in his face." Simon smirked.

Simon slowly opened the door to Vinnie's room and stuck his head inside to see if he was awake.

"Hey, man."

"Simon. Come on in."

"I hope you don't mind." He opened the door all the way. "Grace wanted to come and check on you."

"Hi, Vinnie." I smiled. "I brought you some flowers and a get-well balloon."

"Thanks. What are you two doing here? I hope you got Ives and his guys."

"We did," Simon said.

"They're all dead and sitting in the morgue as we speak." I grinned.

"There was something real sinister about the way you just said that, Grace."

"Sorry. Maybe that's something I need to work on."

"For real though? You got them all?"

"As far as we know," Simon said.

"Even Ives?"

"I emptied my clip into that motherfucker personally," I said.

Vinnie's eyes widened as he looked at me.

"Grace." Simon glanced at me and slowly shook his head.

"Sorry, Vinnie. The doctor said you're going to make a full recovery. That's great."

"Yeah. What about Tommy? He's dead too, right? Cause he's the one who did this to me."

"I shot him right through the forehead." The corners of my mouth curved upward.

"Yeah. While he was holding me hostage." Simon shot me a look. "One millimeter off and it would have gone in my head."

I rolled my eyes. "You're being so dramatic. Isn't he being dramatic?" I asked Vinnie.

"How is that being dramatic? I still can't believe you fired that gun with my head being right there."

"Let it go, Simon. Let. It. Go."

"Thanks for that," Vinnie said. "I can sleep better now knowing they're all dead."

"Anytime, Vinnie. You need someone to disappear, I'm your girl." I gave him a wink.

"Okay. We better get going. We just wanted to let you know that we were thinking about you, and we appreciate everything you've done to help," Simon said.

"Yeah. No problem."

"Come on Grace. Let the poor guy get some rest."

"Call me?" I mouthed to him as Simon pulled me out the door.

"What is wrong with you?" he asked as we walked down the hall to the elevators.

"What?" I cocked my head at him.

"You cannot go around telling people to call you if they need someone killed."

"Please. I was just trying to make him feel better. I didn't mean it. Or did I?" I smiled.

Simon sighed and shook his head as we stepped into the elevator.

The moment we stepped out of the hospital, Simon's phone pinged. Pulling it from his pocket, he read a text message.

"That was from Alex. She invited us over for dinner tonight. Do you want to go?"

"Sure. Sounds like fun."

*S*imon

When I pulled up to my house, my father came walking over.

"Great." I looked over at Grace.

"Hello, Son. Grace."

"Hey, Dad."

"Hi, Henry." She smiled.

"Good God. What happened to both of you?"

"It's no big deal, Dad."

"But it is a big deal." He followed us into the house. "You're still recovering from a gunshot wound."

"Well, I'm done recovering because my captain is letting me go back to work on Monday. Is there a reason you stopped by?"

"Do I need a reason, son? I am your father."

"Sorry, Dad. I'm just a little tired."

"I just wanted to see how you're doing."

"I'm good. I have a lot on my mind."

"It's okay. I understand. I'll go and let you rest." He patted my back. "Take care, Grace."

"You too, Henry. What's going on, Simon?"

"Nothing. He just can't show up whenever he feels like it." I went into the kitchen and grabbed a beer from the refrigerator.

"Why can't he?"

"Because. I love him, but you have no idea what he's put us through over the years with his wives and our mom. We built these houses to get away from him, and now, he's a couple houses down and in all our business. For fuck sakes, he saw you sitting down at the beach, and he had to run over to find out who you were. Now he's got another kid on the way. It's just all too much."

She took the beer bottle from my hand, took a sip, and set it down on the island.

"Listen to me." She gripped my good shoulder. "It doesn't matter what he did, unless he physically harmed you. Did he physically harm you?"

"No. Never."

"Then stop. He's your father and he loves you so much.

Do you know what I'd give right now at this very moment to have my dad come over to see how I'm doing." Tears filled her eyes. "He's worried about you, his son. He could have lost you, and he knows that. Leave the past in the past and cherish every day that he's here with you before it's too late and you live the rest of your life filled with regret."

Cupping her face in my hands, I stared into her beautiful green eyes.

"I'm so sorry for what Ives did to you and your family. You're right. I was acting like a total asshole. Somehow, I feel I can because I think nothing is ever going to happen to him."

"I hate to burst your delusional bubble, but he's human just like the rest of us." A small smile graced her face.

"I know. I'll go over there tomorrow and talk to him." I looked down at her lips as I softly ran my thumb across them.

Leaning in, our mouths met, and our tongues collided. My cock was on the rise, and I wanted nothing more than to be buried inside her again. Breaking our kiss, our eyes met.

"Yeah?"

"Yeah." Her lips formed a smile.

Picking her up, I carried her up the stairs and into my bedroom. I laid her on the bed while I stripped out of my clothes, and she stripped out of hers. The way her taut body looked sprawled over my bed was pure perfection. As she lay there, I ran my finger up her inner thigh until it reached her already wet opening. A soft moan escaped her lips as I leaned in and ran my tongue up and down her, circling her clit until it swelled with pleasure. As my mouth explored her perfectly shaven area, I dipped my finger inside her and listened as her moans grew deeper in sound. She brought her hand to my head and her fingers tangled in my hair while the pleasure I gave forced her into an orgasm. The sweet taste coated my lips, and I couldn't wait to thrust inside her. Running my tongue up her defined torso, my mouth stopped at her luscious breasts and my lips wrapped around her delicate and hardened nipple, while my one hand grabbed her wrist and held her arm tightly above her head.

"I really need to fuck you now." I went to reach over to the drawer of my nightstand, and she stopped me.

"No." The corners of her mouth curved upward. "I have an IUD. I trust you and you can trust me."

Sweet baby Jesus. That was music to my ears.

The corners of my mouth curved upward as I brought my lips to hers and thrust inside her, letting out a gasp at the way her lips tightened around my throbbing cock. Her legs wrapped themselves tightly around my waist. Letting go of her wrist, I drew in a sharp breath as her nails dug into my back. The sexy moans that came from her turned me on even more as my thrusting became faster. I placed my palm against the headboard and rapidly pounded in and out of her until she came. As soon as the feeling hit me, I stopped for I didn't want to come just yet. Rolling her on her stomach, I entered her from behind and gripped her hips. With each deep penetrating thrust, groans rumbled in my chest as the warmth of her coated me. She reached back and grabbed onto my arm, signaling she was about to orgasm again. My heart pounded out of my chest as I was about to explode. One final thrust and the dam opened as I let out a pleasurable moan. Dropping my body on hers, I interlaced our fingers while I tried to calm my racing heart.

CHAPTER 25

*G*race

I lay there in a state of paralysis as gratification soared through my body. His strength, the way he moved, and the sounds of enjoyment that escaped his lips made my entire body melt. He tightly gripped my fingers in his as the warmth of his racing breath swept across the side of my neck.

He rolled off me and fell onto his back. As I lay on my belly, I turned my head and looked at him as I lie there naked. With the slight turn of his head, a smile crossed his handsome face as he reached over and softly stroked the bruise that sat upon my face.

"I wasn't too rough, was I?"

"Not at all." A happy grin crossed my lips. "My body can handle anything."

He let out chuckle. "You shouldn't have told me that."

"Maybe I want you to know." I adjusted my body, so I was lying on my side.

A growl rumbled in his throat as he did the same and his body was aligned with mine. His eyes stared into mine as his fingers brushed a strand of my hair away from my face and a light smile fell upon his lips.

"You look good in my bed."

"I bet you say that to all the women who lie here." I gave him a smirk.

"In all honesty, I've never said that a woman before."

"Are you lying? Because men tend to lie and only tell a woman what they think she wants to hear for their own purposes."

"I agree with that statement, but I'm not lying. You look damn good in my bed."

The corners of my mouth curved upward. "Thank you."

He leaned his head forward and brushed his lips against mine. "You're welcome. We should get dressed. It's almost time to head over to Stefan's house for dinner."

He climbed out of bed and went into the bathroom.

～

"Dinner was delicious, Alex."

"Thank you." A bright smile crossed her face. "I'll pour us another glass of wine and we can take it out to the patio while Stefan and Simon clean up."

"I love that idea." I grinned.

"Yes. You two go ahead. Lily, start clearing the table," Stefan spoke.

"Why?" Her brows furrowed. "Mom said you and Uncle Simon have to clean up the kitchen."

I couldn't help but silently laugh.

"Because I asked you to." Stefan's brow arched.

"How about we negotiate," she said. "I'll take Henry to the living room and play with him while you and Uncle Simon clean up."

He sat there staring at her with a narrowed eye.

"Deal."

Lily got up from the table and took Henry from Simon's arms.

"Come on, Henry. I'll read you a book."

After Alex refilled our wine glasses, we took them outside and sat down.

"You have a beautiful family, Alex." I glanced over at her.

"Thank you. I'll always be grateful for the night Stefan rear ended my car."

"Is that how the two of you met?"

"Yeah. Please don't judge me for what I'm about to tell you." She smirked. "I made a stupid mistake, but out of that mistake I met the love of my life."

"Do tell." The corners of my mouth curved upward.

"I drove from Seattle to California to meet a guy I had met online. The GPS took me some weird way and I ended up turning down a road I shouldn't have. There was this raccoon sitting in the middle of it, so I slammed on my brakes to avoid hitting him and Stefan hit me from behind. I was so mad because I'd had my purse stolen that day with all of my money in it and the guy I was supposed to stay with ended up ghosting me."

"Oh shit, Alex."

"Stefan was kind enough to offer me his spare room for the night and I really didn't have a choice but to take him up on his offer."

"Lily told me you were her nanny."

"I was. Stefan was in-between nannies at the time and offered me the position. The rest is history." She smiled.

"What happened with the online guy?"

"Simon tracked him down and the boys went to his Friday night hangout at the strip club and Stefan beat his ass."

"Good." I laughed. "If I would have been here at the time, I would have done the same thing." I held my glass out to her.

"Thank you. I would have appreciated that." She grinned as she tapped her glass against mine. "Coming into this family was the best thing that has ever happened to me. I love all of them so much."

"What about your family?" I asked.

"My mom died when I was a child, and my father is an alcoholic. I spent my entire childhood taking care of him instead of him taking care of me. The day of my graduation, he didn't show up and when I got home, I found him in bed with my best friend. They were both passed out drunk. So, I packed my things and left. I haven't seen or talked to him since."

"I'm sorry, Alex."

"Thank you, Grace. That's a part of my life I put behind me. Now, I have Stefan and the kids and his amazing family I'm a part of, and I feel truly blessed."

"Hey, Ruby." I smiled as she walked up to me and laid her head on my lap. "How are you, girl?"

"She likes you." Alex smiled.

"I've only met her once since I've been here."

"Dogs know good people."

"There you are," Emilia said as she stepped onto the patio. "I hope she's not bothering you, Grace."

"Not at all. I love dogs and she's a good girl. Aren't you?" I ran my hand down her back.

"Wine?" Alex asked her.

"I'd love some. Thank you."

"I'll go grab a glass." Alex stood up from her seat and went inside.

"Are you okay?" Emilia asked as she pointed to the bruise on my face.

I smiled. "Yeah. I'm fine. Just another day on the job."

"And the person who did that to you?"

"He's buried six feet under."

"Good for you."

Alex walked out and handed Emilia a glass of wine. A few moments later, Stefan and Simon walked out holding guitars in their hand.

"You both play?" I looked at them.

"We do." Stefan grinned. "So does Alex."

"Really?"

"Yeah. And Emilia plays the piano like nobody's business," Alex said.

Simon sat down next to me and strummed his guitar.

"Bro, the D chord is out of tune," Sam said as he and Julia walked over.

"No shit, douchebag." Simon smiled at him.

While he tuned his guitar, Sebastian walked over with his guitar and took a seat next to Emilia.

"What are we playing, Simon? Sam asked.

Simon started strumming the song Sweet Home Alabama.

"YES!" Sebastian grinned as he, Sam, and Stefan joined in, and we all started singing.

CHAPTER 26

*S*imon
    We said goodbye to my family and headed back to my house.

"You were having fun tonight." I smiled.

"I was." A wide grin crossed Grace's face. "Dancing with the girls was the most fun I'd had in a long time."

"I can dance."

"Then why weren't you dancing with us?"

"I prefer something slower." I held out my hand to her with a smile. "Alexa, play Tennessee Whiskey by Chris Stapleton."

The corners of her mouth curved upward as she placed her hand in mine. The song started to play, and we swayed back and forth to the music. Letting go of my hand, she wrapped her arms around my neck as my arm wrapped around her waist.

"I have to admit, Detective Kind, you're a good dancer."

"So are you, Detective Adams. Tomorrow night is the gender reveal party for Julia and Celeste, and you're going with me."

"Are you asking me or telling me?" A smirk crossed her lips.

"I'm telling you."

"Ah, I see. Do you remember when I told you that I don't like people telling me what to do?"

"I remember. Let me apologize for my rude behavior." I leaned in and brushed my lips against hers as my hands gripped her taut ass.

"That's some apology, but I'm not quite convinced you're really sorry."

The corners of my mouth curved upward as I swooped down, picked her up, and carried her up the stairs to my bedroom.

~

*H*er body snuggled against mine as her head lay on my chest while my finger softly stroked her bare shoulder.

"Tell me how you met Connor. If it's too painful to talk about I'll understand."

"It's fine. I was working a murder case at NYU, and Connor was the victim's English professor. I told him I needed to ask him a couple of questions about the victim, and he said he'd answer them over a cup of coffee. I declined because I thought he meant he wanted to take me to a coffee shop or something, but he meant in the faculty lounge."

I couldn't help but chuckle.

"Don't laugh. It was an honest mistake. I thought I got a vibe from him."

"Did you have coffee with him in the faculty lounge?"

"I did. After he answered my questions, we got to talking about different things and then he asked me if I would go on a date with him. At first, I said no but he was so persistent. I never should have married him."

"What? Why would you say that?"

She lifted her head and propped herself up on her elbows, so she was facing me.

"He'd still be alive if I didn't. I carry around this tremendous amount of guilt inside me. And not just because I'm the reason he was murdered, but because I had no business marrying him. I loved him, don't get me wrong. He was an amazing man. I just wasn't in love with him like a wife should be."

I furrowed my brows at her. "Why did you agree to marry him then?"

"Out of loneliness, I guess. I don't know, Simon. Maybe because he was safe. I mean, he was an English professor."

"Since when do you care about safety?" I arched my brow and asked with a smirk.

"You're an asshole." She laughed as she gave me a swift slap on my chest. "I guess I just wanted some normalcy in my life, and I thought he could give me that. And he did for a while."

I could see the pain and agony in her eyes as she lowered her head.

"He would still be alive today if I hadn't been so selfish."

I reached over and placed my finger under her chin and lifted it until our eyes met.

"It was not your fault, Grace, and you need to realize that."

"It doesn't matter what you or anyone else says. It is my fault. An innocent man died because of me, and I'm going to have to live with that for the rest of my life."

Tears filled her eyes, and I wrapped my arms around her and pulled her into me.

"I'm really tired," she said as she broke free from my hold and rolled over.

"Get some sleep." I reached over, turned off the lamp, and then rolled on my side and hooked my arm around her waist. "Good night, Grace." I pressed my lips against the back of her head.

"Good night, Simon."

The following morning when I rolled over, Grace wasn't there. Climbing out of bed, I slipped into a pair of sweatpants and went downstairs. Looking around, I didn't see her, so I stepped out the sliding door and saw her in a meditation pose close to the shoreline. Walking back into the house, I brewed myself a cup of coffee, took it out to the patio and leaned against the rail as I watched her.

"Good morning, son," my father spoke as he stepped onto the patio holding a cup of coffee.

"Hi, Dad."

"What is she doing out there?"

"I think meditating. Listen, I'm glad you stopped by. I'm sorry about yesterday and how I spoke to you."

He placed his hand on my back.

"Don't worry about it. I know you have a lot going on in your head."

"Are you and Celeste excited for the gender reveal tonight."

"Actually, we are. She insists it's a girl, but I think it's a boy. I seem to have a track record as far as producing boys." He smirked and I chuckled. "It's weird that I'm going to have a new son or daughter about the same time as my grandchildren are about to be born."

"I'm not going to lie, Dad. That is fucking weird." I glanced over at him with a smile.

"I noticed your mother has seemed a little down lately. She hasn't been her usual talkative self and throwing jabs at me. Maybe you boys should take her to dinner and find out what's going on."

"I noticed that too. I'll set something up."

My eyes diverted back to where Grace sat on the beach.

"I'm going to head back to the house. I'll talk to you later, son."

"Thanks for stopping over, Dad." I gave him a smile.

"What was Dad doing here?" Stefan asked as he walked over.

"I'm not really sure." I furrowed my brows. "He wants me, you, Sam, and Sebastian to take Mom to dinner. He said she seemed a little down and wasn't her usual talkative self."

"I didn't notice, to be honest. But yeah, let's set a night and we can talk to her about it at the gender reveal party tonight. How are things going with Grace?"

"Good." I smirked.

"Did you talk about what she's going to do now that Ives is dead?"

"No. She hasn't brought it up and neither have I."

"Ignoring it won't make it go away, bro."

"I know." I let out a sigh. "If she wants to leave, there's nothing I can do to stop her."

"Sure, there is." He patted my back. "I have to go and head to the office. I'll see you later."

"See ya, bro."

I finished my coffee and went inside to take a shower for I had my appointment with the psychologist in a couple of hours.

CHAPTER 27

*G*race

For the first time in my life, I had no idea what I was supposed to do. The majority of my life revolved around Ives and avenging my parent's death. Now that it was over, I felt lost, almost as if I didn't have a purpose anymore.

The feelings I had for Simon scared me. I'd never felt the way I did about a man before and that only made me feel worse about Connor. I'd only known Simon for such a short time, and he had an impact on me that was indescribable.

I got up from the sand, dusted myself off, and headed back to the house. When I stepped through the sliding door, I walked over to the Keurig and when I went to grab a k-cup, there weren't any.

"You're back." I heard Simon's voice.

Turning around, I looked him up and down.

"And you look like you're getting ready to leave."

"I have that damn appointment with the psychologist."

"It's not so bad. I've been many times." I smirked. "You'll

be in and out before you know it. It seems you're out of coffee."

"I used the last k-cup this morning. I'll stop and get some more on my way back."

"That's okay. I'll run to the store."

"Are you sure? I can stop."

"I'm sure. I have a couple of errands to run anyway."

"Okay. Thank you. I'll see you later." He gave me a sexy wink that made my heart skip a beat.

I wanted to find an outfit to wear to the party tonight, so I headed downtown to the mall. As I was browsing in Aritzia, I heard a voice from behind.

"Grace?"

Turning around I saw Jenni standing there.

"Hi." I smiled and gave her a hug. "What do you think about this dress?" I held it up.

"I think it'll look fabulous on you. Is it for tonight?"

"Yeah. I wanted something new."

"Good for you. Let's go try it on." She hooked her arm around mine.

"Well, what do you think?" I asked as I stepped out of the dressing room.

"I love it. You definitely need to buy it."

"I think I will." I smiled as I looked at myself in the full-length mirror."

"Do you like sushi?" Jenni asked.

"I love it."

"How about we go get some after you pay for that dress?"

"Sound great. I'm starving."

We walked over to the Blue Ribbon Sushi Bar and Grill and were seated at a booth in the corner. After our waiter brought us a glass of Chardonnay, we placed our sushi order.

"How are you liking Cali?" Jenni asked.

"I like it." I smiled as I picked up my glass.

"Any plans to stick around long-term?"

"I don't know. I'm still trying to figure it all out."

"I feel ya there, sister. I have a lot I'm trying to figure out too."

"Like?"

"I haven't told anyone else this yet, not even Julia. But I'm quitting the modeling business."

"Why?" My brows furrowed.

"I'm getting tired of all the traveling and now with the twins coming, I don't want to miss a thing. Besides, I want to be around more to help Sam and Julia."

"So, what are you going to do?"

"Something I've been wanting to do for a long time." A bright smile crossed her face. "I'm going to start my own fashion label."

"As in a clothing line?"

"Yes! I've been sketching some designs while I've been traveling. A little here, a little there. Mostly on the plane and in the hotel room at night if I'm alone."

"Oh my God. That's awesome, Jenni."

"Thank you. Not a word of this to anyone. I need to find an investor first. I have some startup money of my own, but I'm going to need more. I can't drain my entire savings. Especially if I'm not pulling in a steady paycheck anymore."

"Well, I'm very excited for you." I held up my glass of wine. "May all your dreams come true."

"Thank you, my friend." The corners of her mouth curved upward as she tapped her glass against mine. "How are things going with Simon? Are you still staying with him?"

I bit down on my bottom lip for I'd still felt a little uncomfortable talking about him with her.

"Things are good. And yes, I'm still at his house."

"In his bed, I hope." A sly grin crossed her lips.

"I—"

"It's okay. You can talk about it with me. In fact, I just want you to know that when you hang out with me, Julia, Alex, and Emilia, we're very open about sex with our guys."

"Who are you dating?" I asked.

The grin on her face disappeared as she let out a long sigh.

"At the moment, nobody."

"Come on. You are drop dead gorgeous with an amazing personality. How the hell are you not dating someone special?"

"I go on a lot of dates. Unfortunately, I pick a lot of losers. Except, Simon, of course. He's not a loser in any way. But I just haven't been able to find that one special man who can sweep me off my feet. I don't know." She shrugged. "Julia says I have commitment and trust issues and I look for more cons in the men I date than pros."

"What's his name?" I smirked.

"Is it that obvious?"

"I've been trained to read people and from what I'm sensing, you were in a relationship that ended badly at one time."

"His name was Brendan Koach. I was fifteen and he was sixteen. We met in high school and dated for two years. I was so sure we were going to get married someday. We talked about what kind of house we were going to live in, the number of kids we were going to have, the breed of dog we were going to get, and the trips we'd take. I loved that stupid boy so much that I couldn't see straight. He was my first sexual partner and serious boyfriend."

"What happened?"

"He cheated on me repeatedly. The first time I found out, I broke up with him. Then he got down on his knees and begged me to forgive him. He said it was a stupid mistake and it made him realize how deeply and madly in love with me he was. I believed him, of course. I was a dumb gullible teenager. Less than a year later, he did it again. But I had found out he was having sex not only with one girl, but with multiple girls who were way older than he was. He broke my heart, and I honestly thought I was going to die. I'd never felt such pain in my life. He told me it was my fault he cheated on me. When I asked him how it was my fault, he said I didn't fulfill his sexual needs enough."

"Wow. What a dick."

"Yeah. He certainly was and the funny thing was, his dick was this big." She held up her pinky finger and I let out a laugh. "But I was only seventeen and didn't think about size back then. Now, I do. So, I guess something good came out of it." She grinned.

"You're so bad, Jenni Benton." I held up my glass. "But I one hundred percent agree."

"You never answered my question. Have you slept with the sexy detective yet? Because I'm just here to tell you, if you haven't, you're missing out on a BIG world of fun."

"I'm having fun." I bashfully smiled.

"Good. He's an amazing man, Grace. All the Kind men are. So, give that some thought as you decide whether you're going to stay or leave. But I hope you stay."

"Thanks, Jenni."

We finished the last of our sushi and Jenni looked at her watch.

"I better go. I still have some things to do before tonight." She held up her hand and signaled for our waiter.

As soon as he dropped the bill on the table, I grabbed it.

"Absolutely not." She held out her hand. "Lunch is on me. I was the one who suggested it."

"I know, but I'm paying. I haven't treated a friend to lunch in a long time."

"Next lunch is on me. Got it?" She stood up.

"Got it."

133

Climbing out of the booth, I gave her a hug.

"I'll see you tonight," she spoke.

Suddenly, we heard a gunshot and Jenni screamed as well as everyone else that was in the restaurant.

"Get under the table!" I told her. "Call 911!"

I grabbed my gun from my purse and slowly began walking towards the sound of the shot. When I reached the area by the entrance, I saw one of the waiters lying on the floor with a gunshot wound to his abdomen.

"You," I pointed to a younger man who was under a table close to the waiter. "I need you to put pressure on his wound."

"I'm not coming out." He shook his head in fear.

"Sir, this man will die unless you put pressure on his wound. I am not going to let anything happen to you."

"I'm a nurse." A woman walked over and knelt next to the man.

Another shot was fired, and I quickly followed the sound to the other side of the restaurant where I saw the shooter standing there pointing his gun at an older woman and another man lying on the floor.

"Put the gun down," I spoke.

He quickly turned around and pointed his gun at me.

"Lady, I don't have any beef with you. Don't make me hurt you."

"What's your name?" I asked him.

"What does it matter?"

"My name is Grace."

"Charlie."

"It's nice to meet you, Charlie. What's going on here? Why are you hurting these people?"

"That's none of your business. Like I said, I don't want to hurt you. I'm only here to hurt those who hurt me and my family."

"You have a family, Charlie?"

"A wife and two kids."

"Do you love your wife? Would she want you to hurt people like this?"

"This bitch," he pointed to the woman a few feet from him, "fired me three months ago, and I can't find another job. My wife is sick and now we lost our insurance."

"Then maybe you should have thought about that before coming in late every day," the woman said.

"Shut up!"

"If your problem is with her, why did you shoot two other people?"

"Because they complained about me. They knew my wife was sick."

"Charlie, nobody else has to get hurt. I can help you if you just put the gun down."

"You seem like a nice lady, Grace, but I can't do that."

"Sure, you can, Charlie."

I could hear the loud sounds of the police sirens outside as well as the panic in Charlie's eyes. He looked away and towards the door.

"Charlie, look at me."

He turned his head and his eyes met mine.

"Think of your wife and kids."

"I am!" He became enraged. "They're all I think about! And because of her, my wife won't get better!" he shouted as he quickly pointed his gun at the woman and fired.

I had no choice as I pulled the trigger and Charlie fell to the ground.

CHAPTER 28

*S*imon
        As I was headed home, my phone rang, and
Jenni was calling.

"Hey, you. What's up?"

"Simon." Her voice was low and shaky.

"Jenni, what's wrong?"

"I'm at the Blue Ribbon Bar & Grill. There's someone
here shooting people."

A sick feeling erupted in the pit of my stomach.

"Did you call 911?" I quickly turned the car around and
flipped on my siren.

"Yes," she whispered. "Grace is here."

"Grace is there?"

"We were having lunch. Simon, I'm scared."

"You're going to be okay. Grace won't let anything
happen to you. Put her on."

"She's not here. She grabbed her gun from her purse and
told me to hide under the table."

"Stay put, Jenni. You keep hiding."

I heard a gunshot go off and then another quickly

followed.

I'm on my way."

By the time I arrived, the LAPD and Swat team were already there and inside. When I stepped through the door, Jenni came running over and threw her arms around me.

"Are you okay?" I asked as I looked over her shoulder and saw Grace standing there talking to Roman.

"Yeah. I am now that Grace killed that psycho."

I broke our embrace and walked over to Grace.

"What happened here?" I asked as I placed my hand on her back.

"He got fired, his wife is sick, they lost their insurance, and he came back for revenge. I tried talking to him, but he was too unstable. I had no choice but to fire because he turned the gun on her and fired." I pointed to the woman who was being taken out by the paramedics.

"Grace, I need you to come down to the station for a full statement," Roman said.

"I know the drill. You go home, and I'll be there as soon as I'm done." She placed her hand on my chest.

I gave her a nod and turned to Jenni.

"Are you sure you're okay?"

"Yeah. Just a little shaken, but okay."

I walked her to her car and opened the door for her.

"I can drive you home," I said.

"I'm fine. I'll see you at the party." She kissed my cheek before climbing inside.

After she pulled away, I went back to my car and headed home. Grabbing a beer from the refrigerator, I took it outside and sat down. A few moments later, Stefan walked over holding Henry."

"What are you doing home already?" I asked.

"Lily got out of school early, and Alex had an appointment. So, she dropped Henry off at the office and I went and picked Lily up. Where's Grace?"

"Down at the police station."

"What? Why?" His brows furrowed.

"She and Jenni were having lunch at the Blue Ribbon Bar & Grill and there was a shooting."

"What the fuck? Are they okay?"

"Yeah. They're fine. It was a disgruntled employee, and Grace shot him."

"Thank God she was there." He shook his head.

"Yeah. Good thing. There's no telling how many people he would have killed."

"Dad, I need your help!" Lily shouted. "Hi, Uncle Simon!" She waved.

"Hi, Lily." I smiled as I waved back.

"I have to go. I'll see you later." He held out his fist as he walked past me.

I finished my beer and went back into the house just as Grace walked through the door.

"How did it go?"

"It went good. How was your appointment with the psychologist?" Her lips formed a smirk.

"Like any appointment with a psychologist would go. How did you meet up with Jenni?"

"I ran into her at Aritizia when I was shopping for a new dress for tonight. She asked me to go to lunch with her."

"And we saw how that turned out." I shook my head. "Thank God you were there."

"Yeah. I feel bad for having to shoot him, but he'd already shot three people."

I walked over and placed my hands on her shoulders.

"These things happen. You know there are a lot of unstable people in the world."

"I know. It's just sad. I'm going to take a shower and get ready."

"Okay." I pressed my lips against her forehead.

~

*W*hen we walked into the room at Four Kinds, Sebastian walked over and gave Grace a hug.

"I heard what happened today. Jenni won't stop talking about it. Are you okay?"

"Yeah. I'm good." She smiled.

"After hearing that, I'll think twice about firing someone."

While Grace went over to talk to the girls, I walked over to the table where the spread of food was laid out and where my mother was standing.

"Hey, Mom." I kissed her cheek.

"Hello, Simon." She smiled.

"Sam, Stefan, Sebastian, and I want to take you to dinner on Wednesday. Are you free?"

"That's sweet of you boys, but I'll be out of town."

"Where are you going?"

"Curtis is taking me on a trip to Martha's Vineyard for a few days."

"That's nice. So, everything is okay?"

"Everything is fine." Her brows furrowed. "Why?"

"I don't know. You just seemed a little off last week. I thought maybe you and Curtis—"

"Were having marital problems?" Her brow raised. "We're not. Things are good between us."

"Okay. I'm happy to hear that. We still want to take you to dinner when you get back. Will you let me know what night works for you?"

"Of course, darling." She kissed my cheek. "I'm going to take this plate over to Curtis."

As I was grabbing a strawberry, Sam and Stefan walked over.

"Did you ask her about Wednesday?" Sam asked.

"Yeah. They're going to Martha's Vineyard for a few days."

"Okay. So, things are good between them?" Stefan asked.

"She said they are. I told her we'll get together when they get back."

"Can I have everyone's attention!" Jenni shouted through the room. "Everyone gather round. It's time to find out what two lovely couples are having."

I walked over and stood next to Grace.

"Isn't this exciting?" She smiled.

"Yeah. It's going to be very interesting."

Sam and Julia stood behind two large boxes wrapped in blue and pink polka dot paper with a label that read *Boy or Girl* on each of them, while my father and Celeste stood behind their large, wrapped box.

"Sam and Julia, at the same time, remove the bow from your boxes and lift the lid when we all count to three. One..two..three!" We all shouted.

As they removed the lids to their boxes, pink balloons came flying up from both boxes.

We all shouted and clapped, and Grace glanced over at me with a smile.

"Oh my God, they're having girls!" Stefan laughed. "I love it! I fucking love it!"

"Dad! You said a bad word."

"Sorry, baby. My bad." He patted her head and I laughed.

It was my father's and Celeste's turn as we stood there while the anticipation killed us.

"I bet it's a boy," Sebastian whispered in my ear.

"Another brother?" My brow raised.

"One..two..three!" We all shouted as they lifted the lid and pink balloons flew up out of the box.

"Oh shit. We're going to have a sister," Stefan looked at us in shock.

"Damn. The girls are taking over the family." I smirked.

Excitement and congratulations filled the room as we celebrated.

"I can't believe I'm going to be a father to two girls." Sam smiled as he walked over. "And don't you say a word." He pointed at Stefan.

"What? I think it's awesome." He laughed. "You're going to be surrounded by women and all those hormones. At least I have Henry to balance things out."

Sam reached over and smacked Stefan's chest.

"I still can't believe we're going to have a baby sister," Sebastian said.

"Yeah, I'm shocked too. I thought for sure it was a boy," I said.

Our father walked over, and I hooked my arm around him.

"How are you feeling about having a daughter?"

"It's exciting, son. Celeste and I have been talking about names."

"Did you pick one?" Stefan asked.

"We did. Nora Rose Kind. Nora was Celeste's grandmother's name, and they were very close."

"That's a great name, Dad." Sebastian smiled.

"And you, Sam?" I arched my brow at him.

"We're still discussing it."

"You mean Julia is still deciding." Stefan smirked.

CHAPTER 29

*S*imon

I couldn't catch my breath as she was bent over the bed, and I thrust in and out of her. The pleasure was over the top as I tightly gripped her hips and she called out my name as we both came at the same time. Pulling out of her, she climbed on the bed and fell on her back, placing her hand over her heart as she tried to calm her breathing rate. I climbed on top of her and wrapped my hands around her head as I brought my lips to hers.

"You good?" I grinned.

"I'm good. You?"

"Yeah. Really good. I'm going to hit the bathroom. I'll be right back."

When I was finished, I climbed in on my side and wrapped my arms around her as she snuggled against me. Everything with Grace happened so fast. One moment I was here alone and the next, I had a beautiful woman as my houseguest and in my bed. My mind started to overthink, and anxiety began to set in. I was vulnerable when it came to her, and it scared the hell out of me.

The following morning when I awoke, I stared at Grace who slept there peacefully. Quietly climbing out of bed, I went to the kitchen and made a cup of coffee.

"I didn't hear you get up?" Grace said as she walked into the kitchen and over to the Keurig.

"You were sleeping so peacefully, and I didn't want to wake you. Especially after yesterday and last night. Are you hungry? I can make you some breakfast?"

"I'm good, thanks. Still feeling some of the effects from all the champagne last night." Her lips gave way to a beautiful but small smile.

"Listen, we need to talk." I leaned up against the island with my coffee.

"Okay. What's up?"

"Have you thought about what you're going to do yet?"

"About?"

"Whether or not you're staying in California? I can help you find a place if you decide to stay."

"Actually, I've been thinking about going back to Washington. Unless you think I should stay."

"That's up to you, Grace." I took a sip of my coffee. "Like I said, I'll be more than happy to help you find an apartment or something."

"Why do I get the feeling you're trying to kick me out, detective? That's the second time you told me you'd help me find a place."

"I'm not kicking you out. But you knew this was only temporary, right?"

"Yeah. Of course." Her brows furrowed. "Did you think that I thought I was going to stay here forever?"

"No. It's just—"

"Just what, Simon?"

"I don't want you to stay in California just for me. We had

a lot of fun together, but I go back to work on Monday, and I won't be around as much."

"Yeah. I totally get it. And you're right, I need to figure out what's next for me."

"I'm going to meet my brothers and go surfing. Do you want to join us?"

"No. You go ahead. I'm going to take a shower."

"Okay." I gave her a small smile. "I'll see you when I get back."

"Have fun, and tell your brothers I said hi."

"I will."

~

*G*race

I went up the stairs to my room and started the shower. The moment I stepped in and felt the hot water stream down my body, the tears I'd held back during our conversation fell down my face with full force. Maybe he didn't think he did, but he made it obvious that what we had was over.

As much as I didn't want to admit it to myself, I'd fallen in love with him. I tested him when I asked him if he thought I should stay. If he would have said yes, I would have. But when he told me that it was up to me, I knew right then and there I wasn't important enough for him to make me want to stay. He was a non-committal man, and I was the girl who was afraid to get too close because someone always got hurt. But it happened and now, I was the one who got hurt.

After my shower, I threw my hair up in a ponytail, put on some clothes and quickly packed my things. Looking out the window, Simon and his brothers were still in the water. Grabbing my bag, I walked out the front door and climbed in my car. Once I was out of sight, I sent a text message to Jenni.

"Hey, are you up?"

"I'm up and with a hangover, lol."

"Can I stop by for a few?"

"Yes. Of course. Is everything okay?"

"Not really."

"I'll text you my address and I'll have coffee waiting. Or wine if you need something stronger."

"Thanks, Jenni."

Her address came through, so I punched it into the GPS and headed there. When I arrived at her apartment and lightly knocked on the door, she opened it and gave me a sympathetic look as she saw me holding my bag.

"What did he do?"

I couldn't say anything as the tears started to flow again.

"Come here." She hugged me and then grabbed my bag. "Tell me what happened."

"He said this morning we needed to talk and then he asked if I'd figured out what I was doing. He told me if I decided to stay, he'd help me find a place."

"What?" Her brows furrowed. "That asshole."

"I asked him if he was trying to kick me out and he said no, but he thought I knew our living situation was temporary."

"I'm going to kill him."

"So, I tested him. I told him I was thinking about going back to Washington and I asked him if he thought I should stay."

"What did he say?"

"He said that it's up to me and he doesn't want me to stay just for him. He said we had a lot of fun together, but he goes back to work on Monday, and he won't be around as much."

"UGH!" She clenched her fists. "Don't listen to him,

Grace. He's freaking out because he has feelings for you, and he doesn't know how to handle them. He's never been in this situation before. You have to stay."

"I can't, Jenni. I came here to say goodbye. I have to turn my car rental back in and my flight leaves in a few hours."

"Does he know you're leaving?"

"No. I packed all my things and left while he was surfing with his brothers. Please, don't tell him. I'm begging you. Don't even tell him I was here."

"I won't tell him. Listen, stay with me. I have plenty of room. Once he realizes you're gone, he'll beg you to come back."

"If he was interested and wanted me to stay, he would have told me."

"He's a man and men are fucking stupid. Don't make an irrational decision based on one conversation with him."

"I'm not. You know how he is, Jenni. He can't commit to anyone."

"He can. He just won't." She shook her head. "He might be the most stubborn one of the four of them. But he's different with you. I've seen it and I see the way he looks at you. It's not in a 'I only want to have sex with you' way. It's an 'I'm falling for you, and I can't help it' way. He has issues. I know it, and I think you know it. Please stay."

"I can't. While he needs to figure his own shit out, so do I. I spent a majority of my life going after Ives and now that I've accomplished that, I need to figure out what my purpose in life is now."

CHAPTER 30

*S*imon
    I leaned my board up against the house, took my wetsuit off and went inside. Walking up the stairs, I saw the door to Grace's bedroom was shut so I walked over to it and lightly knocked.

"Grace, can I come in?"

I waited for an answer.

"Grace?" I slowly opened the door and stepped inside.

Looking around the room, I noticed her bag was gone.

"Fuck!" I shouted.

Running downstairs, I grabbed my phone and then opened the front door to see if her car was gone. It was, so I sent her a text message.

"Where are you?"

I waited patiently as I stared at the screen and waited for the bubble and three dots to appear.

"I went up to your room and saw your bag and things are gone as well as your car. You left without saying a word?"

No response came so I threw my phone down on the counter and gripped the edges while I lowered my head.

Picking my phone back up, I sent a text message to Jenni.

"Have you seen or talked to Grace?"

"No. Why?"

"Just wondering. She must have run to the store."

"If she was just running to the store, why would you ask if I'd seen or talked to her? What's going on, Simon?"

"Nothing. I have to run. I'll talk to you later."

My phone pinged and when I glanced over at it, I saw a message from Grace.

"I've decided I'm going back to Washington. Thanks again for letting me stay with you during the whole Ives thing. You're a good friend, Simon, and I'm happy I got to see you again after all these years. Take care of yourself and be safe."

As I stood there and read her message, a sick feeling rose inside me.

"You couldn't have waited until I was finished surfing to say goodbye?"

I waited for the message to be delivered, but it wouldn't go through.

"Wow. Okay, Grace. If that's how you want it," I said out loud as I slammed my phone down.

I ran my hand down my face as I paced back and forth around the kitchen. It was for the best she left. But now, I was going to have to explain to my brothers why. I'd have no choice but to lie to them only because I didn't want to hear it.

Picking up my phone, I called Roman.

"Hey, partner."

"Want to grab some breakfast?"

"Sure. Our usual place?"

"Yeah. I can be there in about thirty minutes."

"See you then."

I ran upstairs and took a quick shower. Grabbing my keys, I climbed in my car and drove to meet Roman for breakfast. When I arrived, he was already there and sitting in a booth.

"Hey, man." He smiled as we did our partner handshake.

"Hey." I slid into the booth.

"I cannot wait to have you back on Monday."

"I can't wait to be back. Anything going on I should know about?"

"Last night another woman was found dead at the Motel 6 in Rosemead. That's the third woman in three months. And here's the thing, all three women were found in different motel 6's and killed the same way.

Any prints or evidence?"

"None. The rooms are always clean. But the woman all have stamps on their hands from the same night club."

"Security footage?"

"This club only has a camera at the door. And on those three nights, the camera went out for exactly one minute."

"Camera footage from the streets?"

"Nothing we could find in the vicinity of the club. But at the three Motel 6 locations, a dark blue van was spotted in the area. Every time, there's a different plate."

"What comes up when you run them?"

"Nothing. They're fake plates. So, when you come back in a couple of days, we need to really move on this case. Speaking of cases, how is Grace?"

"She left this morning to go back to Washington."

"Sorry, boys," Lottie, our waitress walked over and set down two cups of coffee. "We're short staffed and as you can see, we're busy today."

"No problem, Lottie." I smiled.

"You two want the usual?" she asked.

"Yes," Roman and I both answered at the same time.

"I'll go put that in." She gave us a wink.

Roman picked up a pack of sugar and dumped it into his

coffee. "What do you mean she went back to Washington? I thought maybe she'd stay."

"She decided to go back I guess."

"How do you feel about that?" His eye narrowed at me.

"It is what it is." I brought my cup up to my lips.

"Come on, man." He shook his head. "You like her."

"Yeah. I do. She's a great woman. I told her I'd help her find a place if she wanted to stay."

He chuckled. "You kicked her out of your house?"

"No. But she was only staying temporarily."

"You're crazy, man. I know how you feel about relationships, but Grace is different."

"No, Roman, she isn't." I lied. "She said she needed to find her purpose in life now that Ives is dead. Who am I to stop her from doing that?"

"Whatever, partner." He sighed.

"Besides, I'm back at work on Monday, and I won't be around much."

"Okay. Keep feeding yourself a bunch of bullshit."

"Come on, Roman." I cocked my head.

"Hey, I'm just calling it like I see it. But I support your decision, even if I think it's a fucked up one.

$\sim$

*G*race

"There she is." My uncle smiled as he held out his arms.

"Hi, Uncle Aiko. It's so good to see you." I hugged him tight as we stood in baggage claim.

"I was surprised to get your call saying you were returning."

"I missed you." I smiled.

"Well, you may have, but I suspect there's another reason you came back." His brow arched.

We walked to the parking garage and climbed in his SUV.

"The last time we spoke you liked it in California."

I fastened my seat belt. "I do like it."

"And Simon?"

"He basically told me to do what I wanted. So, I came back to re-evaluate my purpose."

"I see. Well, it's good to have you back home. There is something I need to talk to you about."

"Okay." I glanced over at him.

"I've met someone, and we've been seeing each other."

"I haven't been gone that long." I furrowed my brows.

"I met her right before you left, and I didn't want to say anything because I wasn't sure."

The corners of my mouth curved upward. "What's her name?"

"Kim, and she's a wonderful woman. We met at the fish market."

"The one you go to every Wednesday?"

"Yes. She goes every Wednesday as well. I've seen her there for months and we've always smiled and said hello. Then, I got up the nerve to ask her if she would like to have coffee with me. She accepted and we've been seeing each other ever since."

"Wow. Okay." I nodded my head. "I'm so happy for you."

"You'll like her, Grace, and she can't wait to meet you. In fact, she's at the house now."

I arched my brow at him. "Is she living with you?"

"No." He laughed. "But she is cooking for us. She's an excellent cook."

"I can't wait to meet her."

CHAPTER 31

*S*imon

I dreaded telling my brothers about Grace, but I had no choice because sooner or later they would notice she wasn't around. It was seven o'clock in the evening when I walked over to Stefan's house for our usual get-together.

"Hey, bro," all three of my brothers spoke as they sat around the fire pit.

"Where's Grace?" Sam asked.

I grabbed a beer from the table and sat down next to Stefan.

"Bro?" Sebastian asked.

"She went back to Washington this morning."

"What?" Stefan asked. "Why the fuck would she do that?"

"Maybe because she wanted to."

"Bro, I'm sorry," Sam said. "I really thought she was going to stay."

"Yeah, so did I," Jenni said as she stepped onto the patio, walked over and slapped me.

"Damn it, Jenni. That hurt." I furrowed my brows at her.

"Good!" She placed her hands on the arms of the chair

and bent over so our faces were mere inches from each other. "You're an asshole."

"What the fuck?"

"Why don't you tell your brothers why she left, Simon."

"What are you talking about?"

"You know damn well what I'm talking about. She came over this morning on the way to the airport. She told me what you said to her."

"You told me you hadn't seen or talked to her."

"I lied. Just like you're lying to yourself, you egotistical moron."

"Down girl." Julia pulled her back. "Come on. Let's go inside and let the boys talk."

As I sat there, I slammed back my beer.

"Simon?" Sebastian said.

"Damn, bro. What is Jenni talking about?" Stefan asked.

"Yeah. What did you say to Grace?" Sam asked.

"I asked her if she decided what her plan was and I told her if she was staying, I'd help her find a place."

"You kicked her out of your house?" Stefan asked.

"No, douchebag."

"Sounds to me like you did," Sebastian spoke.

"Her staying with me was only temporary and you all know that. Besides, I told her not to stay in California just because of me." I picked at the label on the bottle.

"So, you basically told her to leave town," Sebastian spoke in a stern voice.

"NO!" I shouted as I pointed my finger at him. "She said she needed to find out what her purpose in life was now. Why would I stop her from doing that? What did you want me to do? Force her to stay when she has no clue what she wanted to do? And like any of you can fucking talk."

"You're right," Sam said. "But we learned from our mistakes and we're trying to prevent you from going through the pain and agony like we did because we were too stubborn to admit how we felt."

"I'm not being stubborn. I honestly don't know how I feel about her."

"Bullshit!" Sebastian stood up from his seat and pointed his finger at me.

"Bro, calm down," Stefan said.

"The hell I will."

"Dude, what the fuck is your problem?" I asked.

"You! You're my problem. Grace is the best thing that has ever happened to you, and you will not sit there and deny that. We all see it. We see the way you are with her, and we fucking feel it, brother. I can feel it in my goddamn heart the feelings you have for her. And now, you just let her go like she was nothing! I'm warning you, bro. I better not see another woman coming or leaving your place. Because if I do, I will fucking pulverize you."

"Really?" I shouted as I stood up from my chair. "It's none of your goddamn business who I see or sleep with." I pointed my finger in his face.

"What is going on out here?" Alex shouted.

Sam and Stefan both jumped up from their chairs. Stefan grabbed my arm and Sam grabbed Sebastian's to keep us from punching each other.

I jerked out of Stefan's grip.

"But it was okay for you to do it to Emilia, right?"

"Emilia didn't leave the damn state!" he shouted. "You always have to play this tough guy act and I'm sick of it."

"What the hell is going on?" My father walked over.

"Grace left and went back to Washington because of your dumb ass son!"

"That's it."

I lunged at him and threw a punch to his face. He grabbed me and we both fell to the ground. Sebastian hit me square in the jaw and I took my knee and jammed it in his ribs and pushed him off me.

Sam and Stefan tried to break us up, but my father yelled, "Let them go at it. It's obvious they need to."

Sebastian and I stopped as we both sat on the ground and looked at our father.

"Well, go on. Beat the shit out of each other. Make your father proud."

I glanced over at Sebastian and we both shook our heads.

"I'm out of here." I stood up, grabbed the beer bottle from the table and went home.

Pulling a bag of frozen vegetables from the freezer, I placed it on my jaw. Damn, he hits hard. While I had the frozen bag on my jaw, I poured myself a scotch and took it over to the couch. A few moments later, Sebastian walked into the room.

"Hey."

I looked at him and shook my head.

"You want to finish?"

"Nah. Can you believe Dad said that?" He sat down next to me.

I let out a laugh. "No. I can't." I handed him the bag of frozen vegetables.

"Thanks. He was always the one who broke us up and then lectured us."

"Yeah. I know. I'm sorry I hit you first."

"I'm sorry too, bro. I'm just so mad at you because I know you love her."

"I was lying in bed last night after we had the most incredible sex and suddenly it hit me. The feelings I had for her, how vulnerable I was becoming, and how much I loved having her staying with me. My heart started to race, my mind went into overdrive, and I got scared. Everything I tried to avoid my whole life happened all at the same time."

"I know. Trust me. Sam and Stefan know it too. That's why we tried to help you before it got to this point. We didn't want you to experience the same pain we did because we're four stubborn as fuck morons."

I chuckled.

"She sent me a text this morning and told me she was going back to Washington and thanked me for letting her stay. She told me I was a good friend, and she was happy she got to see me again. I tried to send her a message back, but it wouldn't go through. Obviously, she blocked me."

"Oh shit. I hate when they do that. What are you going to do?" He handed me back the bag and I placed it on my jaw.

"I don't know." I sighed.

"You know, the two of you are two peas in a pod. You're both so much alike. Although, I suspect she's probably a better fighter than you." He smirked.

"She is." I laughed.

"If you would have told her you wanted her to stay, she would have."

"Yeah, I know. I think that's what scared me the most."

"You can always call her from one of the girl's phones. They all have her number."

"I'll give her a couple of days and then I'll do just that. Or I can call her from Roman's phone. He has her number."

"Why does Roman have her number?"

"I'm not sure." My brows furrowed and Sebastian laughed.

"Are we okay in here?" Sam asked as he and Stefan walked in.

"We're good," I said.

"Thank God." Stefan sighed. "I hate it when there's fighting going on."

"Since we're all together, there's something I want to tell you," Sebastian said. "I'm going to ask Emilia to marry me."

"Wow. Congrats." I patted his back.

"It's about time." Sam smiled.

"Congrats, bro. Another wedding."

"When are you asking her?" I asked him.

"I don't know yet. I have to go look at rings first. You three up to coming with me and helping a brother out?"

"I'll go," I said.

"Me too," Sam spoke.

"When are you thinking?" Stefan asked.

"Does Monday work for all of you? I can set the appointment for like five or six o'clock."

"Sounds good," the three of us spoke.

"Just text us the time and place," I said.

CHAPTER 32

MONDAY

*S*imon

"Welcome back, Kind." My buddies all smiled as they took turns patting me on the back.

"Thanks, guys. It feels great to be back behind this desk," I said as I sat down.

"Kind, in my office," Captain Burrows said as he stood in the doorway.

Getting up from my chair, I walked into his office and shut the door.

"Welcome back."

"Thanks, Captain."

"How are you?" he asked as he gestured for me to sit down.

"I'm good."

"I got the report from the psychologist."

"And?" My brow raised.

"She said you're fine."

"I told you I was okay."

"How is Detective Grace Adams?"

"What do you mean?" I furrowed my brows.

"What is she doing now?"

"She went back to Washington. Why?"

"I was just wondering. She's good, but I think she has a problem with authority, quite like someone else I know."

"Yeah. She likes to play by her own rules."

"Anyway, welcome back and stay out of trouble. It's been quite peaceful while you were gone. Let's keep it that way."

"Admit it. You're happy I'm back."

"Get your ass out there. You have a Motel 6 killer to find. In fact, we're going to have a briefing now. Go round up the team."

"Yes, sir."

I rounded up everyone and brought them into the conference room while our Captain went over the case.

"You need to find this guy before he strikes again. The good thing is this guy has a pattern and seems to be killing his victims on the 8th of the month. So, if he continues to go on this spree, we have two weeks until he strikes again. Until then, I want you to find this asshole."

After our meeting, Roman and I headed back to our desks to go over the case.

"The guy is hacking into the motel's system, making himself a reservation using stolen credit cards, and then making his own keycard to get into the room," Roman said. "Once he's finished, he checks himself out online."

"This asshole is just full of talents."

❧

"You're late?" Sebastian said as he cocked his head at me.

"Yeah, bro. And don't even use the excuse about the traffic on I-10. We just came the same way," Stefan said.

"Traffic was a bitch, but it's my first day back at work and I'm trying to find a killer who's going around murdering women with long dark hair between the ages of thirty and thirty-five. So, keep your women out of any nightclubs until this asshole is found."

"Damn." Sam's brows furrowed.

"Good enough excuse for me." Sebastian hooked his arm around me as the four of us walked into the store.

"Hello again, gentlemen." Mr. Rowland smiled. "It's nice to see you all again. Follow me."

He took us back into the same room where Sam and Stefan picked out the engagement rings for Julia and Alex.

"So, which one of you is popping the big question?" He wiggled his finger at me and Sebastian.

"I am," Sebastian spoke.

"Congratulations, young man."

"Don't congratulate him yet. Emilia might say no due to her last wedding disaster." Stefan smirked.

"Really?" Sebastian cocked his head and narrowed his eyes at our brother.

"You're such an asshole." I laughed as I lightly smacked his arm with the back of my hand.

"I know." He gave me a smirk.

"Is there a specific cut of diamond you're interested in? Princess cut, Emerald, Oval, Round?"

"Emerald cut is the square one, right?"

"Yes."

"Definitely Emerald cut and a platinum band.

"I'll go pull some and bring them right in."

"Why Emerald cut?" I asked him.

"It's Emilia's favorite. She was looking online at a ring for her mother's birthday, and she commented on how Emerald cut was the one she always liked the best."

"I sure hope her last engagement ring wasn't that cut," Stefan said.

"It wasn't douchebag. It was oval."

"She told you that?" Sam asked.

"Yeah. I asked her that same night she told me Emerald cut was her favorite."

Mr. Rowland walked back into the room and set six different Emerald cut rings on top of the dark blue velvet cushion.

"They're all beautiful, bro. You're going to have a hard time picking one," I said.

"No. I won't." He pointed to the one in the center. "It's this one."

Mr. Rowland picked up the ring and handed it to Sebastian.

"This is our Tiffany Soleste engagement ring. The center diamond is two carats and the parallel facets down the sides equal one carat making the ring at total of three carats. The diamonds are a flawless cut with exceptional clarity."

"And the price?" Sebastian asked.

"Forty-thousand dollars."

I swallowed hard when I heard the price.

"What do you guys think?" Sebastian glanced at all three of us.

"I think it's perfect." Sam smiled.

"Yeah, bro. It's beautiful, and it'll look stunning on Emilia."

"She's worth every penny, brother." I placed my hand on his shoulder.

"I'll take it."

161

*a*fter the four of us had dinner at Four Kinds, I went home. Pouring myself a scotch, I sat down on the couch and turned on the TV. Grace had been on my mind since the day she'd left and no matter what I did or how busy I was, she was always there. I hadn't slept well the past couple of nights because I missed holding her while she slept. Trying to be tough didn't work out for me very well because the truth was, I needed and wanted her in my life.

I kept thinking back to that day at the beach when we were thirteen years old. I knew back then there was something special about her. And even though we'd only spent a few hours together, I didn't want her to leave. Picking up my phone, I decided to try and send her a text. Maybe, just maybe, she unblocked me. Before sending it, I said a little prayer. I hit the send button and waited for it to say delivered, but it never did.

"Fuck!" I shook my head.

I dialed Jenni.

"What?" she answered.

"I'm surprised you answered."

"I wasn't going to. What do you want, Simon?"

"Come on, Jen. You can't stay too mad at me."

"The hell I can't."

"Can you come over? I need a favor."

She let out a frightening laugh.

"Are you serious?"

"Okay fine. I'm coming to you then and you better answer the fucking door when I get there."

"What the hell do you need, Kind?"

"It has to do with Grace."

"Oh. Okay. I'll be here."

"Thanks, Jenni. I'll see you soon."

When I arrived at her apartment, she opened the door, and I cautiously kissed her cheek.

"If you think that is going to get me to forgive you, it won't."

I let out a sigh.

"I need you to call Grace."

"What?" Her eye narrowed at me.

"I have to see and talk to her. She blocked my number."

"Then that's her telling you she wants nothing to do with you."

"Come on, Jenni. Help your best friend out." I held out my arms. "I miss the fuck out of her."

"Maybe you should have thought about that before you said what you did."

"I know. But you know me, and I don't think right when it comes to women. I'm an idiot."

She stood there with her arms folded and her eyes narrowed.

"It's eleven-thirty where she's at. What if she's sleeping?"

"Text her first and see."

"Fine." She sighed as she grabbed her phone from the coffee table and sat down on the couch.

Taking the seat next to her, I watched as she messaged Grace.

Suddenly, my heart skipped a beat when I saw the cloud and three dots.

"Sure. We can Facetime."

"If she hates me for this, I will never forgive you."

"She won't."

"Don't be so sure, detective."

She hit the facetime button and on the first ring, Grace answered.

"Hey, you." I heard her beautiful voice.

"Hi. I'm sorry to be wanting to Facetime so late."

"No. It's fine. I was just getting ready to go to bed anyway. What's up?"

Jenni went to speak and then paused.

"Jenni, what's wrong?"

"Please don't hate me."

"Hate you for what?" Grace let out a light laugh.

"There's someone here who wants to talk to you."

"Jenni Benton, if it's who—"

CHAPTER 33

*G*race

"Hello, Grace." Simon's face appeared on the screen before I had a chance to finish my sentence.

My heart started to ache.

"Simon."

"I'm sorry for this, and don't be mad at Jenni. I basically forced her to call you. Which by the way, I wouldn't have had to do if you didn't block me."

"I knew you'd be blowing up my phone and to be honest, I just want to be left alone. What do you want, Simon?"

"I wanted to see you and to see how you are."

"I'm fine. I'm where I'm supposed to be."

"I don't think so."

"I have to go."

"Wait, Grace. Listen, can you please unblock me so I can call you on my way home. I'm working on a case, and I could use your advice."

"Why? Why my advice, Simon?"

"Because we're at a dead end and you're really smart. Please, Grace."

"Fine. I'll unblock you."

"Thank you. I'm leaving now, and I'll call you when I get in the car."

"Don't hate me," Jenni said as she took the phone back from him. "I know he's an asshole, but he's hurting now that you're gone."

"I don't care if he's hurting."

A smile crossed her lips. "Yes, you do. I can tell. Anyway, I miss you already and so does everyone else. Sebastian and Simon got into a knock down fight over you."

"What?" I laughed.

"Sebastian went on this rant about what an idiot Simon was for letting you leave, and things escalated. They were on the ground. You should have seen it. I was rooting for Sebastian."

"Who won?"

"They stopped when Henry came running over and actually told them to keep going. They're good now, though. They can't stay mad at each other for longer than five minutes."

"Simon is calling in."

"Okay. Call me tomorrow."

"I will. Hey." I answered Simon's call.

"Hi. Thank you for letting me call."

"So, what's going on with your case?"

"There have been three murders in the last three months. All women with long dark hair, early to mid-thirties, and all killed at three different Motel 6 locations. The guy is meeting them at a nightclub in Los Angeles and somehow getting the women to go with him to the motel."

"Is he drugging them?"

"No. There are no drugs found in their system. Once he gets them to the motel room, he stabs them in the heart and then has sex with them after."

"Jesus. You don't have any evidence of who it could be?"

"No. The room is cleaned except for the victim's blood. He's hacking into the system and booking his own reservation and making his own keycard. Here's another thing. The past three murders have occurred on the eighth of each month."

"The eighth has a significant meaning to him. What about security footage in the club?"

"The club only has one camera at the door and on all three nights of the murder, the camera is out for exactly one minute."

"Sounds like he's hacking into the club's system as well."

"The only lead we really have is a dark blue van in the vicinity of the motels, but each time there's a different plate on it. We have cruisers keeping an eye out for the van on the streets."

"That's not the van he takes the women to the hotel in. He's stealing credit cards to use for the reservations, right?"

"Yeah."

"Is there anything the people who own the cards have in common?"

"No. They're all from different states."

"Wow. This guy is good. Sick, but good."

"There is something that is odd," he said.

"What?"

"The three women who were murdered were all wearing red dresses and red high heels."

"Interesting. He likes the color red. The same color as blood and the heart. That's why he stabs them in the heart. Let me think about this, and I'll give you a call tomorrow."

"That would be great. Thank you."

"You're welcome, Simon. Tell everyone I said hi."

"I will. Good night, Grace."

"Good night."

I ended the call and set my phone down on the night-stand. Bringing my knees up to my chest, I wrapped my arms around them and took in a deep breath.

"Did I hear you talking to someone or am I just losing my mind?" My uncle smiled as he poked his head in the door.

"Simon called."

"Oh?" His brow raised as he stepped inside my room. "And you answered?"

"He called me from Jenni's phone."

"Smart guy." He smirked. "What did he want?"

"He wanted to talk to me about a case he's working on."

"He wanted your help?"

"My insight." I smiled.

"And there it is."

"What?" I gave him a confused look.

"Your smile. I really haven't seen that since you've been back. But now that you've spoken to Simon, it appeared."

"Stop it."

"Just saying, Grace. Get some sleep. I'll see you in the morning."

"Good night, Uncle Aiko."

I let out a sigh as I reached over and turned off my light. As I lay on my back, I gripped the edge of the sheet that was covering me. As hurt as I was by him, it made me smile inside when I saw his face on the screen.

The following morning, I got up, got dressed, and headed outside to my spot under the large oak tree just before the sun was to rise. A tree that had been in that spot for over a hundred years. The locals called it the tree of wisdom, and I believed it because every time I sat under it to meditate things became clearer.

After a while and as I was meditating, I felt something touch my arm. Opening my eyes, I saw a beautiful vibrant green dragonfly peacefully sitting on my arm. I stared at the peacefulness of it and then it flew away. Closing my eyes, I fell back into my meditation.

When I got back to my uncle's house, he was sitting on the porch in his rocker drinking a cup of coffee.

"Are you ready for some training?"

"Yeah. Let me go change first."

After changing, my uncle and I took a walk into the woods and to the open spot he had made years ago to work on our skills.

"While I was meditating, a dragonfly landed on my arm," I spoke as we practiced our moves with each other.

"That's odd. They aren't even around this time of year."

"I know."

"I'm not surprised, though. You're conflicted and unsure. She was there to guide you. What color was the dragonfly?"

"A beautiful green."

"Ah, the heart chakra." He went to hit me, and I blocked him. "The spirit of growth and renewal and—"

"I know. New relationships."

I stopped and lowered my hands.

"Grace, you're an amazing person with a soul and heart made of gold. You deserve to move forward with your life and put the past behind you, all of the past. That's what the dragonfly came to tell you. Great change and transformation are coming your way, but only if you allow it."

I knew all about the dragonfly. My uncle taught me about them and their symbolism and spiritual meaning since I was a kid and we lived in Japan. Going back up to the house, I grabbed my phone and dialed Simon.

"Hey."

"Hi," I spoke. "He was sexually abused as a child. The women represent a type of figure, possibly his mother. She could have been the one abusing him."

"So, you think he's killing women who resemble his mother?"

"Yes. He couldn't actually kill his own mother, but it's his fantasy. He wants to feel like he has control. So, he's playing it out. The color red could symbolize something about his mother. If she wore bright red lipstick or wore a lot of red clothing. She's heartless. That's why he goes for the heart. Do a search in the database for any reported child abuse cases over the last thirty years where the mother was the abuser."

"I will. Thanks, Grace. I appreciate it."

"No problem. How are you, Simon?"

"I've been better. I miss you."

"Don't." I whispered as tears filled my eyes.

"You asked and I answered. I'm not going to lie to you. I have to go. My captain needs to see me. Can I call you later?"

"Yeah. Sure."

"Okay. I'll talk to you soon."

I let out a sigh as I set my phone down.

CHAPTER 34

ONE WEEK LATER

*S*imon
   It was Saturday night and Sebastian invited all of us over for a barbecue. Grabbing my guitar and the beer, I walked over to his house.

"Hey. Do you need any help?" I asked Sebastian who was standing in front of the grill.

"You're funny." He smiled while he pointed a pair of tongs at me.

"Just offering, bro." I grinned as I set my guitar down.

Stepping through the sliding door, I gave Julia, Alex, and Emilia a kiss on the cheek and put the beer in the refrigerator.

"Where's Lily?" I asked Alex as I took Henry from her. "Come to your Uncle Simon, little guy."

"Your dad and Celeste took her to the Beverly Hills Hotel for the night."

"What?" I laughed. "Why?"

"I think he's afraid she thinks the baby is going to replace her. At least that's what Stefan said. He booked a fancy suite, told her they'd order room service, go swimming in the pool, and he even booked her a manicure/pedicure, and a facial for tomorrow morning."

I stood there shaking my head.

"Hey, bro." Stefan walked in and fist bumped me. "Did Alex tell you about Lily?"

"Yeah. What is going on with him?"

"Right?" He laughed. "All we ever got was fifty bucks and told to go play. Let's go sit outside. Unless you ladies need our help?"

"No. We have it handled in here. You two can go." Emilia smiled.

"And take Henry with you," Alex said.

I walked outside and took a seat in the chair next to Sam.

"How's the case going? Did you catch him yet?" he asked as he reached over and let Henry grab onto his finger.

"No. We're working on it. If he stays true to his schedule, hopefully we'll catch the asshole next Friday night."

"How's Grace doing, bro?" Stefan asked. "Have you talked to her?"

"I spoke with her last night. She seems to be doing good."

"Did you ask her to come back?" Sebastian turned and asked me.

"I told her I missed her again, and she told me to stop it."

All three of my brothers chuckled at the same time.

"Well, I hope for our sake she does return because you've been nothing but a miserable douchebag lately." Stefan grinned.

"Aw, leave the miserable douchebag alone," Jenni said as she walked out onto the patio, wrapped her arms around my neck from behind, and rested her chin on my shoulder. "He has no one to blame but himself."

"Thanks, friend. I appreciate your unconditional support."

"You love me, and you know it." She kissed my cheek.

"Who's your latest victim, Jen?" Stefan asked.

"No one now. I'm giving up on guys for a while. I have other things I need to focus my attention on."

"Like?" Sam arched his brow at her.

"I'll let you all know when I'm ready." She grinned and went back inside the house.

"Bro, when is that going to be done? I'm starving," Stefan said.

"When aren't you hungry?" I asked.

"Hey, I have a wife and two kids I'm constantly on the go for. Maybe you should try that sometime and then see how hungry you get."

"You're such a drama queen." I laughed.

He reached over and slapped the back of my head.

"Watch it, bro. I got your kid."

"The food is ready," Sebastian said as he took the chicken, burgers, and hot dogs from the grill and put them on a platter.

As we all gathered at the table, I looked around at my family and took in all the happiness my brothers felt. Julia, Alex, and Emilia were amazing women and Grace was just as amazing. Not only did she fit into my life, but she also fit into my family's life, and to me that was very important.

"Are you okay, bro?" Sam asked.

"Yeah. I'm fine." I gave him a small smile.

After we finished eating, my brothers and I grabbed our guitars and sat out on the patio while we strummed a few chords.

"You first," Sebastian gave me a nod as he sat in the chair across from me.

Jenni stepped onto the patio with Emilia's laptop. "Look who is joining our party!"

She turned the laptop around and Grace was on the screen.

"Hey, everyone." A bright smile crossed her beautiful lips as she waved.

"Hi, Grace," My brothers all spoke at the same time.

"Hi." The corners of my mouth curved upward.

~

*G*race

"Are you going to play for me or what?" I smiled at him.

"Any requests?"

"Whatever you want."

He began to strum his guitar and started singing *Have You Ever Seen the Rain.* The corners of my mouth slowly curved upward as I couldn't take my eyes off him. When he strummed the last chord and sang the last word, I sat there and slowly nodded my head as I lightly clapped my hands and held back the tears that so desperately fought my eyes.

"Damn, bro. That was your best yet," Sebastian said.

I stayed on video chat for a while and joined their party. Laughter and great conversation were mine for the night and they all made me feel like I was there in California with them. I called my uncle over so I could introduce him to everyone, and he stayed and chatted with the guys for a while. After I said my goodbyes, I closed my laptop.

"Those are some great people," my uncle said.

"Yeah. They are." A small smile crossed my lips.

"As much as I love you, Grace, you don't belong here, and I think you know it. Simon even knows it. I watched the way he looked at you. He had the same look in his eyes that your father had for your mother."

"I'm not sure what I know, Uncle Aiko."

"Yes, you do. You just won't let it flow freely inside you because of your fears. I've always taught you that fear is only

174

as deep as the mind allows it. Breathe, let it go, and whatever you do, don't let it decide or control your future. You are stronger than that, Grace. Both physically and mentally. I'll leave you alone with your thoughts." He kissed the top of my head.

~

*S*imon
"You okay, bro?" Sam hooked his arm around me.

"Yeah. I just wish she was here."

"Hey, Roman." Sebastian smiled as he stepped onto the patio.

"Hey, everyone. Simon, can I talk to you alone?"

"Sure."

I got up from my seat and we headed back to my house.

"What's up, partner?" I walked over to the bar and poured us each a scotch.

"We need to talk about something." He gestured we sit down.

"It sounds serious." I furrowed my brows.

"I'm finally working up the courage to tell you what I should have told you a couple days ago, but I just didn't know how."

"Okay. What the hell is going on, Roman?"

"You know I love you, man. You are the best friend a guy could ask for and an even better partner."

"Why do I get the feeling that you're going to tell me you're leaving?"

"I took the test for the FBI, and I passed both the exam and the interview. I start my new position as an FBI agent in two weeks."

"I didn't know you were even thinking about that?"

"I have been for a while. I'm sorry I didn't talk to you about it first. You had been shot and I didn't want to mention it while you were recovering. It's something I feel really strong about."

"I'm not happy about it for me, but I am happy for you." I extended my hand to him.

He pushed my hand away and gave me a hug.

"Thanks, Simon. You have no idea how much that means to me."

"What the hell am I going to do without you sitting across from me and annoying the fuck out of me every day?" I broke our embrace.

"You'll get a new partner to harass. Someone you can mold into a mini you." He smirked.

"Nah., I don't want a new partner."

"You don't have a choice, man."

"I swear to God, if the captain even thinks about putting Billings with me, I'm quitting."

He chuckled. "I don't think the captain is that dumb. There are a lot of great detectives from other districts that are good. Maybe one of them will come over."

"They won't be you, man." I placed my hand on his shoulder. "We've been through some serious shit over the years."

"I know we have, and they've been the best years of my life."

"I'm going to miss you, Roman."

"Stop it, Simon. We'll still see each other all the time."

"It won't be the same."

CHAPTER 35

*G*race

I was sitting under the oak tree meditating when I heard footsteps. Opening my eyes, I stared at the man approaching me.

"Hello, Grace."

"Captain Burrows? What on earth are you doing here?" I stood up from the ground.

"I came to talk to you."

"You flew all the way to Washington to talk to me? You do know I have a phone, right?"

He chuckled. "Yes, I'm aware. When I found out you were here, I brought my wife on a weekend getaway. Our anniversary is tomorrow."

"Is your wife here?"

"She is. She's up at the house with your uncle. He told me you'd be out here. This area is beautiful."

"Yeah. It is." I looked around. "Come on, I'll show you more of it while you tell me why you flew all the way here."

"I want you to come work as a homicide/robbery detective for the LAPD."

"Why?" I glanced over at him.

"Why not? I checked into you, and I spoke with your old captain over at the NYPD. She had nothing but strong words about you. She said you're the best she's ever seen and had the pleasure of working with even though you don't think the rules apply to you."

I laughed.

"I also talked to Jonah Turner, and he told me I'd be a fool if I didn't offer you the position. He speaks very highly of you. Your case records are very impressive. More impressive than Detective Kind's. The two of you worked together to take down Ives, which by the way, I do not condone in any way since he was off duty and on medical leave, and you didn't even work for us. But I was told by the higher ups to drop it. You would be a very valuable asset to the department, Grace, and I think you should consider my offer. Besides, Simon is going to need a new partner since Roman has decided to join the FBI."

"He got in?"

"Yeah. He did. And I'm not sure how Simon is going to take it. Those two are very close. But, if you were to join us, I think he'd take it a lot better. He told me he's been consulting you on the Motel 6 case, and he told me your theory. It's a good one. Unfortunately, we couldn't find anything in the database. We could use your help with this case in California."

"You want me to go undercover in the nightclub to try and find this guy, don't you?"

"Yes. With your certain set of skills, I wouldn't worry too much about you."

"Thanks. I think." I furrowed my brows at him.

"You know what I mean. I saw what you did to the men you put in the hospital."

"You know I was the one who did that?"

"Yeah. I know." He shook his head. "But again, I was told to look the other way."

"Will you also look the other way if I accept your offer and Simon and I become romantically involved?"

He stopped walking and stared at me for a moment.

"You two have already slept together, haven't you?"

"Yep." I smacked my lips together. "And if I come back to California, it will be because I want to be with him."

"Christ on a cracker, Grace." He rubbed the back of his neck.

"If you want me to come work for you, then you're going to have to look the other way, Captain."

"Fine. But you two will need to sign a consensual relationship agreement. After you sign that, I can look the other way." He pointed his finger at me. "But the two of you will not allow your personal feelings to get in the way of your job as detectives. Do you understand me?"

"I understand, and I wouldn't let it anyway. Besides, our relationship will be the least of your worries when it comes to me." I smirked.

"Oh lord. I guess it's a chance I'm willing to take. I have no doubt the both of you will put me in an early grave."

"Aw, Captain." I hooked my arm around him. "You are going to have the time of your life while we're around."

"Somehow, I doubt that. So, are you accepting my offer?"

"I am."

He extended his hand. "Welcome to the LAPD, Detective Adams."

"Thank you." I placed my hand in his and shook it. "Do me a favor and don't tell anyone, including Simon, not yet anyway."

"I won't."

"Shall we head back to the house?" I asked. "I'm sure my uncle is talking your wife's ear off." I smirked.

CHAPTER 36

ONE WEEK LATER

*S*tefan

I could hear Henry crying from downstairs. I thought I was dreaming, but when I rolled over to hold Alex, she wasn't there. Opening my eyes, I climbed out of bed and followed the cries of my son to the kitchen.

"Hey, baby." I kissed her forehead. "Let me take him."

"Thanks. He's teething and I just gave him some Tylenol."

"Okay. Go back to bed for a while, and I'll take care of breakfast for Lily."

"You are my hero. I love you." She kissed my lips.

"I love you too. Okay, little man, I know you're not feeling good, but crying is only going to make it worse." I held him up in the air and he screamed louder.

"Shit. Okay. Okay. Daddy's sorry." I held him tightly against me.

Walking over to the Keurig, I grabbed a mug from the cabinet, popped in a k-cup and waited for the coffee to brew.

"Dad, why is Henry crying like that? He's giving me a headache."

"He's teething, baby girl. You don't have to be up for another half hour."

"Who can sleep with all this noise? Give me him."

My brows furrowed as I handed Henry over to Lily and he stopped crying.

"I'll go rock him in the living room."

"Thanks, sweetheart. I'll make some breakfast. What do you want?"

"Waffles with a berry compote."

"Come on. You know I don't know how to make that."

"Call Uncle Sebastian. He probably already has some in his refrigerator."

"No. You can have plain waffles with syrup."

"Then take your son back. I'm going back to bed."

She handed me Henry and he started crying.

"Fine. I'll call him." I handed Henry back to her, and she took him into the living room.

I let out a sigh as I grabbed my coffee cup and walked over to the sliding door to watch the sunrise before I called Sebastian. A smile crossed my lips when I saw Grace sitting in the sand. Picking up my phone, I called Sebastian.

"Bro, it's too early."

"Look out your sliding door."

"What?"

"Just do it."

"Holy shit. It's Grace. Does Simon know?"

"I don't think so. He would have told us last night if she flew in. By the way, her royal highness wants waffles with berry compote. Do you have the compote?"

"Actually, I do. I'll bring some over."

"Thanks, bro."

After I hung up with him, I called Sam.

"Is this an emergency?" he answered in a sleepy voice.

"Yes. As a matter of fact, it is. Look out your bedroom window."

"Stefan, I swear—"

"Just shut the fuck up and do it, bro."

"Is that Grace?"

"It sure is. I don't think Simon knows she's out there."

"This is excellent, brother. Are you going to call him?"

"Yeah. I'm sure he's still sleeping, or he would have seen her out there."

"I'm going to throw on some clothes and head over to your house."

"Okay. Sebastian is making waffles with berry compote."

"Damn. I'll be right over."

Just as I ended the call, Sebastian stepped through the sliding door.

"Here's the berry compote." He set the container on the island.

"Thanks, bro. Sam is on his way over. I told him you're making waffles."

"What? You didn't say that. You asked if I had berry compote for Lily."

"Well, now we're all going to be here, so start making the waffles."

He let out a sigh.

With my phone in my hand, I dialed Simon.

"What?" he answered in a sleepy voice.

"Why aren't you up yet?"

"I didn't sleep well last night, and I have another forty-five minutes before I have to be up."

"Well, you might want to get up right now and look out your bedroom window."

"Why?"

"Just do it."

"I gotta go, bro. Thanks."

Click.

"I put Henry in his swing," Lily said as she walked in. "Morning, Uncle Sebastian."

"Good morning, your highness. I hear you want waffles with berry compote?"

"I do." She grinned as she walked over to the sliding door. "Is that Grace?" Her face lit up with excitement as she went to open the door.

I grabbed her by her nightgown and held her back.

"No, no, no. You are not going out there."

~

Simon
    I threw on a pair of sweatpants, quickly brushed my teeth, and ran down the stairs. Opening the sliding door, my heart rapidly beat as I walked down to the beach and stood back a few feet from her.

"I thought I was dreaming when I looked out the window."

"Maybe you are," she spoke without turning around.

I slowly walked up and wrapped my arms around her. Bringing her hands up, she placed them on my arms.

"If I'm dreaming, I pray to God I never wake up." I buried my nose in her hair and took in the fresh clean scent that always turned me on. "When did you get in?"

"Around midnight."

"Where did you stay? Wait, let me guess. Jenni's?"

"Yeah. I knew you had to work today so I didn't want to keep you up all night."

"I wouldn't have minded."

She turned around as I held her, and she faced me while her arms wrapped around my neck.

"Simon, I—"

"Shh." I brought my finger up to her lips. "Me first. I'm sorry that I told you not to stay for me. But what I'm most sorry for is letting you go. I should have fought for you to stay, and I should have made you want to stay. But instead, I got scared because the feelings I feel for you are so overwhelming, I didn't know how to handle it. I've never allowed myself to feel the way I do about you. I've spent my life trying to avoid any type of feelings or relationships for fear of failure. As you know, I didn't have the best role models. But what I realized is you bring out the best in me and there's no denying that. I love you, Grace. And I didn't fall in love with you because I was lonely or lost. I was happy living the bachelor life. But when I saw you for the first time twenty years ago on the beach, and then at the warehouse, it was the only time I ever wanted to make a woman a permanent part of my life. And that's what I feared most."

"And now?"

"I have nothing to fear, and you know why?"

"Why?" The corners of her mouth curved upward.

"Because you're the only woman in the world who was born holding the key to my heart."

Tears filled her eyes as they stayed locked on mine.

"I did a lot of meditating when I was in Washington, and my purpose became very clear," she said.

"Which is?" I asked.

"To move to California permanently and love you with all my heart and soul. You, Detective Simon Kind, are my purpose in life, and I'm so in love with you."

I brought my hands up to her face and softly brushed my lips against hers. Swooping down, I picked her up and spun her around.

"Can I take you up to the house?"

"Please do." She grinned. "Are you still offering to help me find a place?"

"I already found you one. It's a beautiful twenty-eight hundred square foot three bedroom three and a half bath home located right on the beach. And the best part about the home are the neighbors. They are the best neighbors anyone could ever ask for. They do tend to be a little nosy, but overall, they're great." I gave her a wink.

"It sounds like a dream home."

"It is. Did I mention the hot guy who comes with the house? He's non-negotiable. You're moving in with me, and I'm not taking no for an answer."

"Is that so?" She laughed.

"Yes. It is. I'll clear some space later. For now, we have something more important to do first."

I carried her into the house and up the stairs.

"Just so you know, I never washed the sheets after you left."

"Why?" She grinned.

"Because I needed to smell your scent every night in order to fall asleep." I kissed her lips as I laid her down on the bed.

CHAPTER 37

*G*race

His hands roamed up and down my naked body while my skin trembled from his touch. His mouth explored my neck before making its way down to my breasts, and my back arched the moment he dipped his fingers inside me. He knew what I loved, and he wouldn't stop until I orgasmed. I was close with each pleasurable moan that escaped my lips, and he knew it. His mouth met mine and our lips tangled as I swelled beneath his touch.

"That's it, baby. I've missed this so much."

My moans grew with intensity as my body shook and a pleasurable orgasm tore through me. He broke his lips from mine and his tongue slid down my body. My fingers tangled in his hair as his mouth explored me. I threw my head back in delight as my back arched, begging him to go deeper. As much as I enjoyed his mouth all over me, I needed to feel him inside me. I placed my hands on each side of his face and forced him to look up at me. He slowly climbed on top of me and as his body hovered over mine, he thrust inside me.

"Is this what you want?" A smile crossed his lips.

"Yes. Oh God, yes," I moaned.

After a few thrusts, I pushed him off me and he rolled on his back. Straddling him, I placed my hands on his muscular chest and slowly lowered myself until the full length of him was buried inside. We both gasped in sync as gratification and pure bliss overtook us. My hips moved back and forth in a steady motion as his hands stroked my breasts.

"You are so sexy," he spoke with bated breath. "God, I love seeing you this way."

I leaned down and smashed my mouth against his as I continued to grind on him. With him still buried inside me, he rolled me on my back and began to rapidly thrust in and out of me like a wild beast who hadn't had a meal in weeks. My heart rapidly beat out of my chest as the feeling rose and the pressure built. My body shook with delight as my legs tightened around his waist. Throwing my head back, I let out a moan as bolts of electricity flowed through me. His groans became louder as he slowed his thrusts, and I felt the warmth inside me. His heated body collapsed on mine while we both lay there and tried to catch our breath.

"I love you," he whispered in my ear.

"I love you, too," I whispered back as my arms tightened around him.

He lifted himself up and off me, rolling onto his back and grabbing my hand and interlacing our fingers. Bringing my hand up, he pressed his lips against it.

"I don't want to go to work and leave you."

"You have to go work. People need you. Besides, I need you to drop me off at the car dealership on your way to the station."

"You're buying a car?"

"I already bought it. I just need to pick it up."

"When did you do that?" he asked with a smile.

"A couple of days ago. So, come on. You get in the shower, and I'll make the coffee."

"What kind of car did you buy?"

"You'll see." I gave him a smirk.

~

"Can I help you?" the perky redhead sitting behind the large, curved desk asked.

"I'm looking for Mike Rogers."

"May I tell him who's here?"

"Grace Adams."

While I waited for Mr. Rogers, Simon walked around the showroom and looked at the cars on display.

"Miss Adams, it's a pleasure to finally meet you in person." He extended his hand.

"It's great to meet you, Mike. This is Detective Simon Kind."

"Nice to meet you, detective."

Simon gave him a nod as he shook his hand.

"Well, your beauty is waiting for you outside. Are you ready?"

"I am." I grinned.

We followed him outside, and I smiled as I saw my new car sitting there looking pristine in all its glory.

"Wait a second. You didn't." Simon looked at me as we approached my brand-new Porsche 911 Turbo S Cabriolet in the color black.

"I did."

"Damn, Grace." He walked around the car and examined it.

"Here are your keys." Mr. Rogers handed them to me. "It was a pleasure doing business with you Miss Adams. Enjoy your new toy."

"Oh, I will." I smiled as I opened the door and climbed inside.

Rolling down the driver's side window, Simon leaned in and slowly shook his head.

"What?" I laughed.

"I'm trying to decide which is sexier, you or the car."

My jaw dropped as I reached over and slapped his arm.

"You know I'm teasing. I love you, you sexy thing." He chuckled as he leaned in and kissed my lips.

"I love you too. I'll see you later."

After putting the top down, I peeled out of the parking lot."

CHAPTER 38

Simon

"She's quite a woman," Mr. Rogers said as we stood there and watched Grace quickly drive out of the lot.

"Yes, she is, and she's all mine." I smiled as I glanced over at him.

I climbed in my car and drove to the station. When I walked in, Roman was sitting at his desk.

"You're late," he said.

"I have a really good excuse."

"What is it?"

"Grace is back." I smiled.

"Say what? Congratulations, partner." He held up his hand for a high-five.

"Thanks. She showed up this morning and of course I had to properly welcome her back." I smirked.

"Of course. I would be worried if you didn't."

"Kind, in my office," my captain shouted as he stood in the doorway.

I sighed as I got up from my seat and walked over to his office.

"What is it, Captain?"

"I want to talk to you about your new partner."

"Listen," I put my hand up. "I don't want to discuss that now. I'm not ready to have Roman replaced."

"That's too bad. Your new partner is here and it's time you met. Detective Kind, meet your new partner." He gestured with his head.

Turning around, I stood there in shock when I saw Grace in the doorway.

"Howdy, partner." A bright smile crossed her lips.

"Wait—what?" I turned to my captain. "Grace is my new partner?"

"She is."

"But—"

He put his hand up. "I already know. I need you both to sign this consent form to cover my ass in case the two of you decide one day to kill each other."

"I can't believe this." I smiled as Grace walked over and stood next to me.

"Are you mad?" she asked.

"Mad? Hell no. I'm beyond happy to have you as my new partner."

"Just do me a favor and keep your public affection out of the office," Captain Burrows said. "She's not your official partner yet. Not until next week, but she is helping us tonight with the case."

"What do you mean?" I furrowed my brows.

"I'm going to the club tonight and hopefully our killer will be there."

"Grace is our best option. She'll wear a red dress and red heels. If he's there, he'll notice her."

"When did you plan all this?" I cocked my head at my captain.

"When I paid Grace a visit in Washington to offer her a

position here."

"Why didn't you tell me any of this?" I asked Grace.

"I wanted to surprise you. Plus, I had some things to get in order first."

~

I wasn't sure how I felt about Grace being the bait tonight. I knew I didn't have to worry about her, but I couldn't help not to. She left the station and told me she'd meet me at home later. My brothers had texted me and asked if I could meet them at Emilia's for a quick lunch.

When I stepped through the door, I went straight to our family table and saw my brother's already sitting down.

"We're happy Grace is back," Sam said.

"Thanks, so am I?"

"We were all watching the two of you this morning from my house." Stefan smirked.

"I knew you were. Nothing gets past any of you. I'm surprised Dad didn't come running out."

"We called and warned him to leave you two alone." Sebastian smiled.

"Thanks for that." I chuckled. "You're never going to believe this, but Grace is my new partner."

"Duh," Stefan said.

I picked up a French fry from my plate and threw it at him.

"My partner at the station. She's replacing Roman."

"What?" Sam asked. "Is that even allowed if the two of you are in a relationship?"

"Captain Burrows made us sign a consensual agreement. Apparently, he flew to Washington to talk to Grace and offer her the job."

"Wow. I think that's awesome," Sebastian said as he lifted

his glass. "To our brother, his new girlfriend, and his new partner."

"Thanks, bro." We all tipped our glasses to each other. "She's going undercover tonight at the club. We're hoping the guy will be there looking for his next victim."

"Ha. He isn't going to know what hit him when she gets through with him." Stefan smirked.

$\approx$

*G*race

I emerged from the bathroom and did a little twirl as Simon sat on the edge of the bed staring at me.

"Wow. Just wow." He stood up and walked over to me.

The corners of my mouth curved upward. "You like what you see?" I wrapped my arms around his neck.

"What do you think?" A smirk crossed his lips as he pressed his hard cock against me.

"Now is not the time, you bad boy. Can you help me with this wire?"

"Are you seriously going to leave me with a case of blue balls?"

"I will take care of them later. Right now, we have a killer to catch."

He let out a sigh as he put the wire on me, and then we met the rest of the team in a van that was parked down the street from the club.

"Are you ready for this?" Roman asked.

"I'm ready."

Simon looked at me and firmly gripped my shoulders.

"You better be careful, and I mean it." Worry consumed his eyes.

"I will be."

"Try not to break any body parts." He smirked.

"I can't make any promises when he pulls that knife on me." I gave him a wink and headed down the street to the club.

Once I was inside, I went up to the bar and ordered a cosmopolitan. Taking a seat on one of the stools, I turned around so I could scan the crowd. Between my long dark brown hair, vibrant red dress, matching heels, and bright red lipstick, if he was here, he wouldn't be able to miss me.

"Anything yet?" I heard Simon's voice in my earpiece.

"Not yet." I continued to scan the crowd.

My eyes locked onto a man's who stood at a distance staring at me. Around six foot three, jet black hair and taste-fully dressed. He began walking towards me as I sipped my drink.

"Tall, dark, and handsome man around early to mid-thirties is approaching."

"Hi." He flashed his pearly whites.

"Hi."

"I'm sure you hear this from a lot of guys, but I couldn't help but notice how stunningly beautiful you are."

"Thank you. I appreciate your kind words. Obviously, my ex-boyfriend didn't feel that way since he decided to break up with me."

"Then he's nothing but a fool. May I buy you another drink?"

"I'd love for you to." I gave him a flirtatious smile. "But I think I should know your name first."

"Mark." He extended his hand. "And you are?"

"Grace." I placed my hand in his.

"Are you here alone or are you waiting for someone, Grace?"

"It's just me."

"A beautiful woman like yourself shouldn't be in a place like this alone. There are a lot of weirdos out there."

"I'm not alone anymore, am I?" The corners of my mouth curved upward.

"No. You're not. I would be more than happy to keep you company tonight. Unfortunately, I'm leaving town in the morning. I'm only here on business."

"What do you do?" I asked as I sipped my cosmopolitan.

"I work for a technology firm as an Information Security Analyst."

"Interesting."

"May I ask what you do?"

"I'm in the modeling business. But I'm currently in-between jobs."

"I can totally see you being a model." He placed his hand on my knee. "Your dress is beautiful. Red is my favorite color, and it looks gorgeous on you.

"Thank you." I bashfully smiled. "Mine too."

"So, you said you're in town for business. Does that mean you're staying at a hotel?"

"Actually, I am. It's nothing special since the company I work for is fairly cheap."

"I'm sure it's nice. Maybe I can judge for myself." I placed my hand on his right thigh.

"Easy, Grace." I heard Simon's voice.

"I'd love to take you back to my hotel room. Shall we?" He threw some cash down on the bar.

CHAPTER 39

*S*imon
   As I sat in the van with the crew and listened to every word this guy said, a sick feeling settled in my stomach. The two of them walked out of the club just as a cab pulled up to the curb.

"We checked all the cab companies and there was not one that drove to any of the Motel 6's," Roman said.

"He must be manipulating their system. Call that cab company right now," I said to Vince.

We followed them to the Motel 6 in Inglewood and watched them go up to room 205.

"I told you it wasn't anything special. I'm kind of embarrassed to even bring you here. Someone as beautiful as yourself deserves more luxury." I heard him say.

"No. It's fine."

"Why don't you get on the bed and get comfortable. I'm going to use the bathroom."

"Of course. Don't take too long," Grace said.

*G*race

Before laying down on the bed, I checked underneath it and under the mattress for a knife.

"I can't find the knife," I whispered to Simon and Roman.

"He probably has it in the bathroom. That's why he went in there. Be careful, Grace," Simon said.

I heard the knob turn so I quickly jumped on the bed and laid down, tucking my gun underneath the pillow. Mark stepped out completely naked with one hand behind his back.

"Wow," I said as he stood at the end of the bed. "You didn't tell me to get undressed."

"That's because I want to undress you myself." He slowly climbed on top and straddled me. "I hope that's okay?"

"Yeah. Sure." I smiled.

"Can you do me a favor and place your hands above your head and close your eyes?

"Why?" I asked.

"Because I said!" A switch flipped and his demeanor changed. "I'm sorry. I didn't mean to shout. Please do as I ask. I promise you're going to love it."

"Okay." I lifted my arms above my head and closed my eyes.

"Now keep them closed for me. I'll tell you when you can open them."

I felt his body slightly shift and when I opened my eyes, I saw the shiny six-inch blade coming at me. I grabbed his wrist with both my hands and twisted it until he dropped the knife.

"This is your idea of seducing a woman, you sick fuck!" I yelled as I grabbed his ear and pulled him off me.

He fell to the ground, and I quickly swung my legs

around the side of the bed and kicked him in the face with my heel, sending him flat on his back.

"You stupid bitch!" he shouted as he tried to grab my leg and I kicked him again.

Grabbing the gun I hid behind the pillow, I cocked it and pointed it at his man parts.

"LAPD. One move and I swear I will blow it to pieces."

The door forcefully opened and Simon and Roman ran inside.

"Are you okay?" Simon looked at me and then down at Mark.

Placing his hand on mine, he lowered my gun.

"I'm happy you used control and didn't blow it off."

"I wanted to." I raised my brow.

"I know you did, babe."

Two officers cuffed Mark, dressed him, and threw him into the back of a police car.

"Good work, Detectives." Captain Burrows walked in.

"Thanks, Captain," I said.

"We'll get the knife to the lab and make sure it's the same one that was used on the three victims. In the meantime, you two go and get some rest and I'll see you in the morning."

When we stepped into the house, I kicked off my shoes while Simon poured us a drink.

"Here's to catching a killer." He held up his glass. "I think I'm going to like having you as a partner." A smirk crossed his lips.

"I think I am too." I grinned as I pressed my mouth against his.

We heard the sliding door open and when we turned around, we saw Sam, Stefan, and Sebastian walk in.

"How did it go?" Sam asked.

"Damn, Grace." Stefan smiled. "You look—"

"Finish that sentence and see what I do to you, bro." Simon pointed at him.

"We're happy you're back." Sebastian walked over and gave me a kiss on the cheek.

"Thank you. It's good to be back. The night went great. I didn't get stabbed to death, a killer was caught, and now he's behind bars. Drink?" I asked the boys.

"Nah. We just wanted to stop by to welcome you back and to see how it went," Sam said.

"Thanks for stopping by," Simon said. "But I need some alone time with my girlfriend."

"We get it, bro." Stefan grinned. "Enjoy the rest of your evening, and we'll talk tomorrow."

"You are surfing with us in the morning, right?" Sam asked.

"I don't—"

"Yes. He is." I smiled. "I'll make sure he's up and out on the water."

"Why don't you join us?" Sebastian asked. "I have an extra surfboard."

"Thanks. But maybe next time."

CHAPTER 40

*S*imon

"Did Sebastian ask Emilia to marry him yet?" she asked as I held her tightly against me.

"No. He was going to, but her birthday is next weekend and he's taking her on a trip up to the cabin in Bear Lake, so he's going to do it there. Can I be honest with you about something?"

"Of course." She lifted her head and rested her chin on my chest.

"I didn't think you were ever coming back, and I was going to have to go to Washington and kidnap you."

"That's hot." The corners of her mouth curved upward. "Now I kind of wish you would have."

"I was thinking about it."

"I could always go back, and you could kidnap me." She grinned.

"Nah. It wouldn't be the same. What are you going to do with your time before you officially start as my partner?"

"Well, my stuff will be arriving in a couple of days. So, I'll have some unpacking to do. I can cook dinner for you every night and have it ready for when you walk through the door."

"Really?" My brows furrowed. "You don't seem like that type."

"I was kidding. I'm not." She let out a laugh.

I pulled her on top of me and held her face in my hands.

"I'm so in love with you, Grace."

"I'm so in love with you too, Simon." She smiled as she pressed her lips against mine.

The following morning, I got up, put on a pair of board-shorts, kissed Grace on the forehead while she slept, and headed down to meet my brothers.

"You made it." Sebastian smiled as he held out his fist.

"You knew I would." I bumped my fist against his.

Stefan walked over and out of nowhere, threw his arms around me and pulled me into an embrace.

"What's wrong, bro?" I patted his back.

"Nothing. I'm just happy to see you so happy."

"Okay." My brows furrowed as I looked at Sam and Sebastian. "Thanks. I appreciate it."

"Now that I got that out of the way, let's go hit some waves!" Stefan shouted and grabbed his board from the sand.

As we were out in the water, I looked over and saw our father sitting in the sand watching us.

"This is creepy," I said.

"What the hell is he doing?" Sebastian asked.

"It's kind of uncomfortable," Sam spoke.

"Maybe he's just watching us because—hell, I don't know. I wish he wouldn't."

We paddled back to shore and took our boards out of the water. After grabbing our towels, we walked over to where our father sat.

"Morning, Dad. Whatcha doing?" I asked.

"Watching my boys surf. Is that a problem?"

"No. Not at all," Sam said.

"What's wrong, Dad?" Stefan asked.

"Yeah. We can tell something isn't right," Sebastian spoke.

"I got a call last night that an old friend of mine passed away."

"Gee, Dad. We're sorry," I said.

"When was the last time you saw him?" Sam asked.

"It was a woman, and I haven't seen her since before you boys were born."

"Oh," Stefan said as he looked at us.

"How did she pass?"

"Massive heart attack."

"Who called to let you know?" I asked.

"A friend of mine. He had heard from someone who knew her."

"Did she live around here?" Stefan asked.

"No. She actually lived in New York."

"We're sorry, Dad." Sebastian patted him on the shoulder.

"Thanks, boys. Listen, I know I haven't been the best father in the world over the years, but I did try."

The four of us furrowed our brows at each other.

"Between your mother and I, we did a pretty good job at fucking the four of you up as far as relationships are concerned. Thank God, your women straightened your asses out. And you too, Simon. I'm happy Grace is back."

"Thanks, Dad. Me too."

"You only fucked us up a little bit," Stefan said, and I reached over and smacked him.

"It's okay. You can admit it, and I will take full responsibility. But I'm going to do right by your sister."

"And we'll be there to help you," Sam spoke.

After my father went back to his house, I invited my brothers over for a cup of coffee.

"What the hell do you think all that was about?" I asked them.

"I have no idea," Sam said.

"I think his friend's death got to him. Maybe because it made him think of himself and the possibility he could die at any time," Sebastian said.

"Are we overlooking the fact that his friend was a woman from New York?" Stefan asked.

"Mom and Dad used to live in New York before we were born," I said.

"I know that. But don't you think it's odd that if she was a 'close' friend, he would have kept in touch with her after they moved out here?"

"What are you saying, bro?" Sebastian asked.

"I'm just saying what if she was a lover or something."

"Come on. I don't think so," Sam spoke.

"Really, brother?" I chuckled.

"Think about it for a second. He hadn't seen or spoken to her since before we were born. Yet he called her a 'close' friend. Just doesn't make sense, and knowing Dad, he was probably cheating on Mom with her and that's why they moved across the country."

"Or he was cheating on her with Mom." Sam's brow raised.

"Nah." Stefan shook his head.

"It doesn't matter," I said. "Let's leave it alone. You guys can stay and finish your coffee if you want, but I'm going up to see my beautiful girlfriend." I gave them a smile and a wink and headed up the stairs.

CHAPTER 41

ONE MONTH LATER

*S*imon

"Are you ready?" I asked Grace as I wrapped my arm around her waist.

"I'm ready."

"We're taking your car today, and I'm driving." I grinned.

"We took my car yesterday. Are you paying for the gas?"

"I got you." I gave her a wink.

She threw me the keys and we headed out the door.

We were already halfway downtown when she dug through her purse.

"Shit."

"What's wrong?"

"We need to stop at the store."

"For what?"

"I forgot to put tampons in my purse, and I need chocolate."

"Seriously? You need that now, right this second?"

"Yes, right this second. I need to change it when I get to the station. Why are you being so dramatic over stopping at the store?"

FOUR OF A KIND

"I'm not. We're going to be late."

"We'll be fine. I'll buy you a Red Bull and a glazed dough-nut." The corners of her mouth curved upward."

"You sure know the way to a man's heart." I grinned.

I pulled into a 7-Eleven, and we went inside the store. I headed to the refrigerated section to grab a Red Bull while Grace went to find some tampons and chocolate. Suddenly, I heard a loud voice.

"Empty the drawer, now!"

I ducked down, looked around, and saw Grace carrying a box of tampons as she crawled over to me.

"I swear to God, I'll shoot you! Open the safe!"

"Really?" I cocked my head at Grace.

"What? Like I knew the place was going to be robbed." We both pulled out our guns.

I looked up at the mirror affixed to the ceiling and took note of the two men with guns and one cashier.

"You really needed tampons this second? The women's bathroom has one of those machines on the wall."

"And you know this how?" she asked as we slowly walked towards the front.

"I just do."

"Uh-huh. We'll talk about that later."

"LAPD! Drop your weapons now!" I shouted.

The two men turned around and pointed their guns at us.

"Don't make me shoot you," Grace said. "I'm on my period and I'm cranky. Tell him, Simon."

"She's right. Totally cranky and a little bit psycho. You don't want to mess with her."

"We ain't afraid of no bitch cop on her period."

"Shit. Now you're in trouble. You shouldn't have called her that."

Before he could pull the trigger, Grace kicked the gun out of his hand, did a sweep kick to his leg and he fell to the floor. When he went to get up, she hit the back of his head with her gun.

"Stay down," she told him.

The other guy jumped over the counter and held the cashier at gunpoint.

"I'll kill him."

Grace and I stood there with our guns pointed at him.

"What a way to start the morning," I said. "If only you would have remembered to put some tampons in your purse, we wouldn't be here."

"Maybe if you didn't distract me in the shower this morning, I wouldn't have forgotten."

"What the fuck is wrong with you two?" The guy with gun frowned.

"Should I?" She glanced over at me.

"Just don't kill him," I said.

"What?" He cocked his gun and Grace fired hers, shooting him in the leg.

He went down and I jumped over the counter and kicked his gun away from him.

"She shot me!" he screamed as he held his leg.

"I warned you she's a little psycho." I grabbed his hands and cuffed him while Grace called it in.

"Are you okay?" Grace asked the cashier.

"Yeah. I'm fine. Thank you. Thank God you two were in here. Anything you want is on the store."

"Really?" Grace smiled as she set her box of tampons on the counter and two Hershey bars.

I grabbed my can of Red Bull and a glazed doughnut from the case and set them on the counter.

"Grab a doughnut for the captain," Grace said.

"Why?"

"Trust me. We'll need it."

I reached in the case and pulled out another glazed doughnut.

"Are you paying or what?" I asked her.

"He said we could have anything we want."

"Yes. You are forever in my debt," the cashier said. "You saved my life."

"See, we saved his life." She smiled.

I pulled out a twenty and threw it on the counter.

"Is that enough?" I asked him.

"That's fine. But really, you don't have to."

Two cop cars showed up within minutes and Larry and Carla walked in.

"That one behind the counter needs medical attention. The ambulance should be here shortly."

"It looks like this one does too," Larry looked up at us.

"Nah. He's just knocked out." Grace said.

"Can we get to the station now?" I arched my brow at her.

"Yes." She grabbed the bag from the counter.

"You're filling out the report on this one," I said as we climbed in her car.

"Why?"

"Because you're the reason we had to stop."

"You just won't take any responsibility for anything, will you?"

"Nope." I grinned as I took off down the road. "But you know I still love you, right?"

"Yeah. I know." She smiled as she placed her hand on mine.

When we walked into the station, Grace handed me my Red Bull and my doughnut. Just as we both went to sit down at our desks, our captain shouted, "Kind and Adams, get in here."

"Yes, Captain," we both spoke at the same time.

SANDI LYNN

"What the hell happened at the 7-Eleven? Who is responsible for shooting the suspect in the leg?"

"I am," Grace said as she handed Captain Burrows his doughnut. "He had the cashier at gunpoint, and he cocked his gun. I had no choice."

"What's this for?" he asked.

"I thought you'd like one." Grace grinned.

"And the other guy who was knocked out cold?" His brow arched.

"He called her a bitch," I said.

"Yeah. That's a trigger word for me." She scrunched her face.

He let out a sigh as he ran his hand down his face.

"Fill out the report and get it to me ASAP."

"I'm on it, Captain," Grace said.

"By the way, thanks for the doughnut."

"You're welcome. See, I told you we'd need it," she whispered in my ear when we walked out of his office.

I glanced at her with a smile and shook my head.

CHAPTER 42

*S*imon
The four of us were sitting in the living room at Stefan's house while the girls were in the kitchen baking cookies with Lily. It was a stormy night in Venice Beach, so we couldn't sit outside.

"How are the two peas in the pod doing?" Stefan grinned.

"Are you referring to me and Grace or Sam's twin girls?" I furrowed my brows at him.

"You and Grace, idiot."

"We're great." I smiled. "Why?"

"Just asking. I love to see you with that smile on your face instead of the resting bitch face you used to sport."

Sam and Sebastian chuckled, and I threw my bottle cap at Stefan.

"Speaking of two peas in a pod, I can't believe how big Julia is."

"I know." Sam sighed. "And she's so uncomfortable. I wish I could do something for her. I've been doing all the cleaning lately."

"I bet you have." Stefan rolled his eyes and I snickered.

"Hey, did you see the Bennett's are moving out?" I asked. "I saw a moving truck in their driveway this morning."

"Yeah. I saw that," Sebastian said. "I talked to Jerry last week and he didn't say a word about them moving."

"I wonder who's moving in," Stefan said. "I hope for your sake they're cool people." He pointed at me.

"Yeah. Me too. And I hope they're quiet."

"Well, we aren't the quietest neighbors. So, you really can't complain if they're not," Sebastian said.

"True." I raised my brow as I tipped the bottle to my lips.

The women walked into the room and when I looked over, I saw Grace holding Henry.

"There's your Uncle Simon." She walked over and handed him to me.

"Come here, little man." I held him up and he smiled.

"You're so good with him."

"I have experience." I gave her a smirk. "I helped Stefan a lot with Lily when he was a single parent."

"And you're going to get a lot more with the twins and our little sister." Sam smiled.

"That's for sure, my brother."

⁓

"Simon, help me. Help me, Simon. I need your help."

"Simon, wake up. You're having a nightmare." I felt the shaking of my shoulder.

My eyes flew open as my heart pounded out of my chest and I was drenched in sweat. Quickly sitting up, I ran my hand down my face.

"Are you okay?" Grace asked as she switched on the lamp.

"Yeah."

"You were having a nightmare. What was it about?" She placed her hand on mine.

Once I was able to calm my breathing, I turned my head and looked at her.

"It was about Drew. I could hear him calling me for help, and I couldn't find him."

"Come here." She wrapped her arms around me and pulled me into her.

"It was so real, Grace."

"I know." She pressed her lips into the top of my head. "It was only a dream."

The following morning, when I got out of the shower, Grace stood there holding a towel and a cup of coffee in her hands.

"Thanks." I leaned in and kissed her lips as I wrapped the towel around my waist and took the cup of coffee from her.

"Are you okay?"

"It's been a long time since I dreamt about Drew. I don't even know why I did."

"Sometimes, they have a way of reaching out for a reason. You better hurry up or we're going to be late." She reached up and kissed my lips.

~

*W*e were sitting at our desks talking over a case when Captain Burrows walked over.

"A woman just called and said her contractors were tearing out one of the walls and found a hammer wrapped in a piece of cloth inside her fireplace. She said it looks like there's dried blood on it. Cruz and Kim are already out on another case. So, I need you two to check it out." He handed me a piece of paper with an address on it.

I looked at the address and swallowed hard as my heart started racing.

"Let's go." I stood up from my chair and looked at Grace.

"What's wrong?" she asked as I walked ahead of her to the elevator.

I handed her the piece of paper.

"That is the address where Drew used to live when we were kids."

"What?" Her brows furrowed.

"Drew died from a blow to the back of his head. His body was found in the woods twenty miles north from his house."

"You don't think that—"

"I don't know what to think right now."

We pulled up to the house and knocked on the door.

"Can I help you?" a middle-aged woman asked when she answered the door.

"I'm Detective Kind and this is Detective Adams with the LAPD." I showed her my badge. "You called in a hammer that your contractor found inside one of your walls?"

"Yes. Please, come in. It's right there on the table." She pointed.

I pulled a glove from my pocket, put it on my right hand, and picked up the hammer to examine it.

"My contractors found it when they were taking down the wall in the living room. We had no idea there was a fire-place behind there."

"How long have you lived here?" Grace asked.

"We just bought the house six months ago. We're putting windows in on each side to brighten up the room."

"Do you have a plastic bag?" I asked her.

"Yes. I'll go grab one."

"Drew's father was a contractor and I remember when he was redoing this room. His mother hated the fireplace and told Drew's dad she wanted it out. I remember being over one day and hearing them fight about it."

We took the hammer back to the station and down to the lab.

"Hey, Mitzi." I smiled.

"Hey, Simon."

"I need you to test this ASAP."

"How fast? I'm backed up right now."

"I need it now. Please, Mitzi. This is personal."

"Only for you." She smiled. "I'll get working on it now."

"Thank you. I owe you."

"I'm going to hold you to that, Detective." She grinned.

When I got back to my desk, I ran my hand over my face and let out a sigh.

"Talk to me, Simon," Grace said as she sat across from me. "Were there any problems at home that you know of?"

"Just the usual arguing here and there. Nothing major. Drew was missing for a week before they found his body. I remember going over to his house to talk to his mom and his dad had already put up the drywall to cover the fireplace. I asked her why he did that, and she said he needed to keep busy because he couldn't handle that his son was missing.

"So, you think the father killed him?"

"I have no idea, Grace, but that's what it's looking like. Where Drew was found, a sixteen-year-old girl was also found in the area a couple months before. She was raped and then strangled. The police searched for a year to find the person who did it, but there was no evidence. A couple years later, another body was found, and the man was caught. He confessed to killing the sixteen-year-old girl, but he claimed he knew nothing about Drew. Six months after his death, his parents sold the house, packed up, and moved to New York."

"Why would they move to New York?"

"His mom told me that it was too painful to stay in California and she couldn't handle it anymore."

A few hours later, Mitzi called to let me know she had put the report into the system. Pulling it up, I read it as tears filled my eyes.

"The small specks of blood that were on the hammer definitely was Drew's." I looked at Grace.

"I think it's time we pay Drew's parents a visit in New York," Grace said.

"I agree. Can you check and see when we can get a flight out? That's if you want to go. You don't have to, Grace. I can go by myself."

"I want to go, Simon. Besides, I won't let you do this by yourself." Her lips formed a beautiful smile. "All the flights are booked for today, but there are two seats left in first class that I can book for tomorrow morning at eight-thirty."

"Book them. I'll go talk to the captain."

After I explained everything to Captain Burrows, he told us it was fine, and we could go. In all honesty, I didn't give him much of a choice.

CHAPTER 43

*S*imon

When we got home from work, I sent a text message to my brothers asking them to come over around eight o'clock. Grabbing the bottle of scotch and four glasses, I took them outside on the patio while Grace packed her bag.

"What's with the emergency meeting?" Sam asked as he sat down, and I handed him a glass of scotch.

"Yeah, bro. What's up?" Stefan asked.

"I'll tell you as soon as Sebastian gets here. He's on his way home from the restaurant."

"Come on, bro. Now you've got us worried," Stefan said.

"There's nothing to worry about."

Sebastian walked onto the patio and took a seat next to me. Pouring him a glass of scotch, I handed it to him.

"Thanks. What's this about?"

"Grace and I are flying to New York tomorrow to talk to Drew's parents."

"Why?" Sam's brows furrowed.

"A hammer with Drew's blood on it was found stuffed in the fireplace of his old house."

"The one that his dad covered up with drywall?" Sebastian asked.

"Yeah. Some new owners bought the house six months ago and they were tearing out the wall to put in a couple of windows. They had no idea there was a fireplace behind the wall. The contractors found the hammer wrapped in a cloth."

"Shit," Stefan said. "You're not saying that Drew's father had something to do with his death, are you?"

"It kind of looks that way, bro."

"No. No way." Sam shook his head. "He would never do that. He was the nicest guy."

"And his mom was the sweetest woman I knew," Stefan said.

"Can't really say that about Drew's sister, Maggie. She was always a psycho bitch," Sebastian said.

"Yeah," Sam said. "Remember when she was on the swim team and Nadine Trumball accused her of trying to drown her because she scored better than Maggie did?"

"I think that was just Nadine being a drama queen. Those two always had it in for each other," Stefan said.

"What about when she was caught shoplifting and went crazy and punched out the security guard," Sebastian said.

"Oh yeah. I remember that," Sam said. "There was always something off with her."

"Are you sure his parents still live in New York?" Stefan asked.

"Yeah. I did a search and got their address. They live in Manhattan."

After my brothers and I talked for a while, they left, and I headed up to bed. When I walked into the bathroom, I wrapped my arms around Grace from behind as she stood there brushing her teeth.

"I think Drew's older sister killed him and his parents covered it up."

She stopped brushing and stared at me through the mirror.

"Why do you think that?" she asked before she rinsed her mouth.

"Just a gut feeling."

"How much older was she?"

"They were thirteen months apart. Let's get some sleep. We have to be at the airport early."

We both climbed into bed, and I hooked my arm around her as she laid her head on my chest.

"Are you sure you're okay with going back there?" I asked.

"Of course, I am. Stop worrying about me. Besides, I wouldn't let you go alone anyway."

"I hate to break it to you, Grace, but you're going to have to let me worry about some things when it comes to you. That's what boyfriends do."

"Fine. If it makes you feel better to worry, than go right ahead." She lifted her head and brushed her lips against mine.

"Which hotel did you get us again?" I asked her.

"The Mandarin. I have a friend who works there, and he's giving me a great deal." The corners of her mouth curved upward. "Plus, it has amazing views of Central Park and comfy beds."

"You know this, how?" I arched my brow at her.

"I just do." She gave me a wink and laid her head on my chest. "Go to sleep, detective. I love you."

"I love you too, but we're not done discussing how you know that the bed is comfy."

"Stop being so dramatic."

~

"*C*an I help you," An older woman asked as we approached the reservation desk at the Mandarin.

"We're checking in. The reservation is under the name Adams. Grace Adams."

"Well, look who the cat dragged in?" I heard a man from behind say.

Grace turned around with a smile on her face.

"Silas. It's good to see you." She gave him a hug.

"Good to see you too, detective. What brings you back to New York?"

"A case we're working on. This is Detective Simon Kind. Simon, this is Silas. He manages this fine hotel."

"It's nice to meet you, Silas." I extended my hand.

"Nice to meet you too, Detective Kind. I have to run, Grace. Enjoy your suite."

"I will, and thanks again."

"You're welcome." He gave her a wink, and I narrowed my eye.

"I saw that." She smiled. "Be nice."

"Are you going to tell me how you know him?"

"I know a lot of people in this city, Simon." She smirked and reached up and kissed my lips.

~

*W*e walked up to the apartment building at West 76th Street and took the elevator up to the fourth floor.

"You okay? You're fidgeting," Grace asked as she placed her hand on my back.

"I'm fine."

After a couple of knocks, Mrs. Canfield opened the door.

"Can I help you?"

"Hello, Mrs. Canfield."

"I'm sorry but do I—" She cocked her head as she stared at me. "Simon?"

"Yes. It's me." The corners of my mouth curved upward.

She reached out and gave me a hug. "Oh my gosh. It's so good to see you again. Come in."

"It's good to see you too, Mrs. Canfield. This is my girl-friend, Grace."

"It's nice to meet you, Grace. Please, have a seat." She gestured to the couch in the living room. "I just made a fresh pot of coffee. May I get you two a cup."

"That would be great. Thank you."

"I'd love some." Grace smiled.

Within moments, she returned with a tray which carried three coffees and a small plate of chocolate chip cookies.

"You're in luck, I just made a fresh batch of chocolate chip cookies. I remember they were always your favorite, Simon."

"I knew I smelled them when I walked in."

"Harry just ran out to the store. He's going to be thrilled when he sees you." She brought her hands together and placed them over her mouth while she stared at me. "Look at you. You are such a handsome young man. How are your brothers?"

"They're great. Sam is married with twins on the way, Stefan is married with a daughter and son, and Sebastian just got engaged. Oh, and my father remarried, and he and his wife are expecting a little girl."

"Good lord. I can't even imagine starting over at that age. How is your mother doing?"

"She's good. How's Maggie doing?" I asked.

"Maggie is doing well. She's married now, and she's a freelance graphic designer."

"She always was a good artist," I said. "No grandchildren yet for you and Mr. Canfield?"

"Unfortunately, no. Maggie has decided she never wants children." She set her coffee cup down on the table. "My goodness. I can't believe it's been over twenty years since I saw you last. What are you doing for a career?"

"I'm actually a homicide detective with the LAPD."

"Is that so?" Her expression went flat. "Do you enjoy it?"

"I do. I love my job very much."

"I thought you were going to work for your father's company."

"That was the plan initially until Drew was killed."

She started fidgeting with her hands and became extremely nervous. The front door opened, and I heard footsteps in the hallway.

"Harry, we have a visitor and you're never going to believe who it is."

He stepped inside the room and stared at me for a moment.

"Simon Kind?" He cocked his head.

"Hi, Mr. Canfield." I smiled as I got up and we hugged.

"My god, look at you. You're all grown up. How are you, son?" He patted my back.

"I'm good," I spoke as I sat back down.

"Harry, Simon is a homicide detective with the LAPD."

"Really? Good for you, Simon. That's a very important job. What brings you all the way to New York?"

I inhaled a sharp breath as Grace pulled a couple pictures from her large purse.

"Actually, I came to talk to you about this." I set the pictures side by side on the table. "There's been a development in Drew's case. This is the weapon that killed Drew, and it was found buried in the fireplace you covered up after he went missing. Any idea how it got there?"

"I have no idea." Harry could barely speak the words. "How do you know that hammer was used to kill my son?"

"The blood found on it, matches Drew's, Mr. Canfield. As well as the tiny specks that were found on the cloth it was wrapped in."

"Your first mistake was keeping the murder weapon," Grace said. "But you were hoping someone would find it someday. That's why you put it in that fireplace."

"I think you both need to leave," Harry said. "Right now. Get out of my house right now."

"We're not leaving until you tell me why you killed your son," I said.

"How dare you come into my home and accuse me of such a thing!" he shouted. "You have no right, Simon. I loved my boy, and I would never hurt him!"

"Then who did? Who are you covering for? Maggie? Did Maggie kill Drew?" I shouted back. Grace reached over and placed her hand on my arm.

He went silent and fell back in his chair. Placing his face in his hands, he slowly shook his head.

"Harry, don't." Mrs. Canfield squeezed his arm.

"It's too late, Darcy."

I looked at Mrs. Canfield as tears streamed down her face.

"Too late for what?" I asked.

"Maggie was a troubled child. You knew that. We were out to dinner with some friends and left Maggie to look after Drew. She and Drew had gotten into an argument, and she snapped." He started to cry. "When we got home and saw what she had done, Darcy begged me not to call the police. She said she couldn't lose both of her children."

"Harry, stop!" she cried.

"I wrapped Drew's body in the area rug we had in the living room we were redoing and put him in the back of my pickup truck. I had remembered that a sixteen-year-old girl was found in that wooded area about twenty miles north and the killer hadn't been found yet. So, I took my son out there to make it look like he had killed another child. When I got home, I wiped Maggie's fingerprints from the hammer, and I thought I had wiped off all the blood. After I wrapped it in a cloth, I threw it it inside the fireplace and put the drywall up."

"I called the next morning to say goodbye because my dad was taking us up to Bear Lake for a week and you said Mrs. Canfield had him up early to run some errands with her and that you'd tell him I said goodbye. But you didn't report him missing until the next day."

"I knew nobody was going to find him out there so quickly, and we needed to come up with a plan on what we were going to tell the police. We knew that he was planning to meet Danny Southers at the beach that day. When Danny called to tell him a time, Darcy said he was in the bathroom and she'd tell him, and he'll meet him there. The cops wouldn't let us report him missing until twenty-four hours had passed. I called them and told them Drew never made it to the beach and we were worried. It took us six months to get everything in order to move here. And the only reason we did was because we put Maggie in an excellent psychiatric care facility where she got the help she needed."

"She's a devoted Christian and she married a wonderful man. She's a Sunday school teacher as well. She's repented for her sins, Simon," Mrs. Canfield cried.

"How could you? She murdered your son!" I shouted.

"You don't understand because you don't have children. A parent would do anything to protect their child," Mrs. Canfield said.

"What about Drew?! Why weren't you protecting him?" I stood up from the couch and pointed my finger at them in anger. "She murdered your son in cold blood!" I shouted.

"My best friend! And you two covered it up as if Drew meant nothing to you! Grace," I looked over at her.

She got up from the couch, walked over to the door, and two police officers stepped inside.

"I couldn't lose both my children!" Mrs. Canfield screamed.

"You wouldn't have! Maggie would have got the care she needed and been out when she turned eighteen, and the two of you could have continued to live out your lives." I shook my head. "Now, you're going to jail and so is Maggie. Get them out of here," I said to the two police officers who hand-cuffed the Canfield's.

CHAPTER 44

*G*race

"It's over." I hugged Simon tight as Maggie was escorted out of her apartment in handcuffs.

"I never would have found his killer if those people hadn't wanted to put in some damn windows."

"It doesn't matter, Simon. It's over, and now Drew can finally rest in peace."

I took hold of his hand and led him over to where Peter, an officer I worked with at the precinct, stood.

"Can you do me a favor and drop us off at the Mandarin Hotel."

"You sure you don't want to come down to the station? Everyone would love to see you again. You heard about Carrie, right?"

"Heard what?" I played dumb as my brows furrowed.

"Carrie was killed last month. She and her partner were working on a case with the FBI and things went sideways during a raid."

I glanced over at Simon and noticed him staring at me.

"I didn't know that. Wow. I'm sorry."

224

"Yeah. It's quite a loss. Anyway, climb in and I'll give you guys a ride to your hotel."

"You know what?" Simon said. "Thanks, Peter, but we're going to catch a cab. I have somewhere else I want to stop first."

"You do?" I cocked my head.

"Yes. I do," he spoke with seriousness.

"Okay. Suit yourselves. It was good seeing you again, Grace. Come back and visit."

"Yeah. Maybe I will. Thanks, Peter."

Simon took hold of my hand and began walking me down the street until we hit the intersection.

"Did you kill her?" he asked.

"Who?" I looked over at him.

"Your ex-partner, Carrie."

"How could I? I was with you in California when she was killed."

"Did you know she was killed?"

I took in a deep breath and didn't answer his question.

"Grace?"

"Yes," I quietly spoke.

"So, you lied to me." He held up his hand to get us a cab. "Again."

"No. But I did lie to you about something else."

I watched as he inhaled a sharp breath.

"Breathe, babe. Breathe." I placed my hand on his chest as the cab pulled up.

⁓

*S*imon
     The cab ride to the hotel was silent and when we got back to the room, I fell back on the bed and placed my hands behind my head.

"Are you going to tell me what you lied about?" I spoke in an authoritative tone.

"Are you going to keep being so dramatic about it?" Her brow raised.

"Grace, I swear to God. I'm in no mood."

"I knew Carrie was the mole. Tommy was paying her off for information. She was the one responsible for Connor's death because she knew I would be out that night he was killed. She was also responsible for Tommy getting off on a technicality and she was feeding him information about things we'd found out. That's how they were always one step ahead."

"And you didn't take her out?"

"No. And just for the record, I have no control over what the FBI does." I looked away from him.

"So, the FBI knew she was mole?"

"Yes."

I let out a sigh.

"Come here." I held out my arms.

"No. I don't want to be anywhere near you when you have an attitude like this."

"I don't have an attitude. But answer me this, is there anything else you need to tell me before it pops up out of nowhere one day?"

"No. I've told you everything."

"Are you one hundred percent sure?"

"I swear on my life and my uncle's life."

"Come here then."

"Why?" Her eye steadily narrowed at me.

"Because I need you and that sexy body."

A wide grin crossed her lips. "Since you put it that way." She jumped on the bed and straddled me.

"I love you," I spoke as I brought my hand up to her cheek.

"I love you too." Her lips met mine.

FOUR OF A KIND

After we had some fun and took a little nap, we went downstairs to the bar for a couple of drinks before dinner.

"Grace, long time no see." The bartender grinned as we took a seat on the stools.

"Hey, Pauly." She leaned over the bar and kissed his cheek. "This is my handsome boyfriend, Detective Simon Kind of the LAPD."

"It's nice to meet you, Simon." He extended his hand.

"It's nice to meet you too, Pauly."

"You have your hands full with this one."

"Don't I know it." I smiled.

"She'll always keep you on your toes."

"She already does." I chuckled.

"Okay." Grace laughed as she put up her hand. "You can stop talking about me."

"What can I get you, Simon?"

"Single malt scotch, 17 year."

"Excellent. I already know what you want." He gave Grace a wink.

He poured my scotch and set Grace's martini with two olives down in front of her, then walked away to help other customers.

"How do you know him?" I asked

"He's a retired firefighter, and his wife is a dispatcher for the NYPD."

"And now he works here?"

"He does it part time. It's more of a hobby for him. I was hoping he was working tonight."

"I need to hit the bathroom. I'll be right back." I kissed her cheek. "Don't pick up any strange men while I'm gone."

"I'll try my best, Mr. Kind." She smirked.

After washing and drying my hands, I opened the door and headed back to the bar. That's when I noticed a tall and good-looking guy around the same age as I was dressed in a designer suit talking to Grace. I wasn't pleased and ready for a fight.

"There you are." Grace smiled. "He thought I was his blind date."

"Really?" I arched my brow at him as I pursed my lips.

"I'm sorry. You probably thought I was trying to hit on your girlfriend. I swear to God I wasn't." He held up his hands. "I'm supposed to be meeting a woman named Selena. It's a blind date and all I know is she said she has long brown hair and she'll be wearing a black dress. When I saw Grace sitting here alone, I thought she was Selena, my blind-date."

"Okay. It was an honest mistake," I said.

"By the way, I'm Shaun." He extended his hand.

"Simon." I shook his hand.

"It's nice to meet you, Simon. Even if it's under awkward circumstances." He frowned.

"Nah, man. It's all good." I patted his shoulder.

"Can I get you something, buddy?" Pauly asked him.

"I'll have a single malt scotch, 17 year."

"You have great taste in scotch." I held up my glass.

"Wow. You too." He grinned.

As soon as Pauly set his drink down, Shaun pulled out some cash from his pocket and handed it to him. "This covers my friend's drinks as well."

"You don't have to do that," I said.

"I want to. I feel stupid enough as it is. Anyway, it was nice to meet you both. I'm going to sit over there and wait for my blind date who is fifteen minutes late already. Never a good sign." He shook his head.

"It was great to meet you too," Grace said. "He seems like a really nice guy."

"Yeah. He does. A lot nicer now that I know he wasn't hitting on you." I arched my brow.

"Stop it." She smiled.

We finished our drinks, and I looked at my watch.

"We need to get going if we're going to make our dinner reservation."

"Good. I'm starving." Grace grabbed her purse.

We both stood up from the stool and I glanced over to where Shaun was sitting.

"Look at that. His blind date finally showed."

"Oh, she's pretty," Grace said.

"Not as pretty as you are. Poor guy." I smirked. "He's probably thinking the same thing."

"You're sweet, but evil."

"I'm evil?" I said as we walked hand in hand out of the hotel. "You're the one who seeks people out and breaks their limbs before you interrogate them."

"You know what? You wait until we get back to the room later. You're going to pay for that remark, mister."

"Promise?" I smiled as I gave her a wink.

CHAPTER 45

*S*imon

We checked out of the hotel early so Grace could stop by the cemetery to visit Connor's grave before heading to the airport. When we arrived, she set down the flowers I'd bought for her to give him.

"Hey, Connor."

"I'll give you some privacy." I placed my hand on the small of her back.

"No. It's okay. You can stay. I don't want to be here long," she spoke. "I got him, Connor. I killed the man who took your life. I know you don't see him because he's in Hell and you're up with the big guy. But you can rest in peace now knowing he's exactly where he belongs." She brought her index and middle finger up to her lips and then placed them on his headstone. "Rest in peace, my love."

I hooked my arm around her and pulled her into me.

"I'm ready to go," she spoke in a soft voice.

"Okay. Let's go home, babe." I kissed the side of her head.

We boarded the plane and took our seats in first class.

"May I get your something to drink?" the flight attendant asked us.

"I'll have a mimosa," Grace said. "Light on the juice."

"I'll have a scotch." I smiled as I shook my head.

"What?" Grace asked.

"Nothing, babe." I leaned over and kissed her lips.

I pulled out my phone and sent a text message to my brothers in our group chat.

"Grace and I are on our way home. See you tonight."

"Good. You've only been gone two days and I already miss your douchebag ass," Stefan replied.

"Happy to hear it, bro. See you later," Sam said.

"Family dinner at the restaurant tonight. Seven p.m."

"Are you going to tell us which one or do we have to take a guess and risk showing up at the wrong place?" Stefan asked.

"Four Kinds, douchebag."

I let out a laugh.

"Family dinner at Four Kinds tonight. You up for it?" I asked Grace.

"Totally up for it." She grinned.

"We'll be there, my brothers."

"Simon. Grace?"

We both looked up at the same time.

"Shaun? What are you doing here?"

"I'm on this flight. In fact, I'm in this seat." He put his bag up in the overhead and sat in the aisle seat across from me.

"It's good to see you again, Shaun." Grace smiled.

"Good to see you too, Grace. Wow. How weird is this? Are you two going to California on business as well?"

"No. We live there," I said.

"No shit? What a small world. I'm headed there for a couple of days for business."

"What do you do?" Grace leaned over and asked.

"I'm in capital investment. What about you two?"

"We're both detectives with the LAPD," Grace said.

"Detectives? Nice. Were you two just on a romantic getaway to the Big Apple?"

"No. Actually, we were here following up on a case," I said.

"Well, I hope it was worth it."

"It definitely was." I smiled.

The flight attendant walked over and handed us our drinks.

"Welcome aboard. Can I get you something to drink?" she asked Shaun.

"I'll have a scotch."

"So, how did your blind date go last night?" I smirked.

"It was okay. Nothing exciting. She just wasn't my type."

"Poor girl. I hope you let her down easy," Grace said.

"I didn't have to. I don't think I was her type either. We both mutually agreed to cut the evening short."

"Aw, I'm sorry."

"Don't be, Grace. I know there's someone special waiting for me somewhere in this big world. I'll find her someday."

The flight attendant handed Shaun his drink and I held my glass out to him.

"Touché, my friend."

He smiled as he tipped his glass to mine.

As we were exiting the plane, I asked Shaun if he needed a ride.

"Do you need a ride somewhere? We'd be more than happy to drop you off wherever you're headed."

"Thanks, Simon, but I have a car and driver waiting for me. It was great to see you two again. Thanks for making the flight a good one." He smiled.

"Take care, Shaun." I patted his back.

"Bye, Shaun." Grace waved to him. "He's such a nice guy."

"Yeah. He's pretty cool."

There was something about him that seemed very familiar to me, but I couldn't put my finger on how or why.

"You're back!" Stefan grinned as he gave me a hug when we stepped inside the room at the restaurant.

"Hey, bro."

"Welcome home," Sam grabbed my hand and pulled me into a bro hug.

"Hey, Simon. Welcome back," Sebastian said as he also hugged me.

"Uncle Simon!" Lily came running over. "I'm happy you're home."

"Me too, Lily. Me too." I hugged her tight.

I looked around and didn't see Jenni.

"Where's Jenni?"

"She's going out with her model friends tonight for someone's birthday."

We all took our seats at the table and enjoyed the excellent dinner Sebastian and his staff prepared for us.

"I cannot believe Maggie killed Drew and his parents covered it up," Sebastian said. "I told you she was a psycho bitch." He pointed his fork at me.

"Yeah. I know you did, bro."

"I'm happy it's finally over," Stefan hooked his arm around me. "You can put it behind you now."

"I am. Knowing that the entire family is behind bars, gives me peace of mind."

"And peace for Drew," Sam said as he raised his glass. "To Drew. May his soul rest in eternal peace. Cheers."

"Cheers," We all toasted him.

After we finished eating, Sebastian brought out a variety of tarts for dessert.

"Damn, bro. These look delicious," Stefan said as he grabbed one.

"Which one do you want?" Grace asked.

"I'll take the lemon." I smiled.

"Good choice. But I'm going for the chocolate." She smirked.

"It's almost that time, isn't it?"

"It sure is." She grinned as she shoved a spoonful of chocolate tart in my mouth.

"Hey, Sebastian?"

"Yeah, bro?" He walked over. "Do you have any more of these tarts I can take home?"

"I have some more in the back. Which ones do you want?"

"The chocolate." I winked at Grace.

"I'll have Maria box some up for you."

"Thanks." I grinned.

After he walked away, Grace smacked me. "You are so bad."

"What?"

"I know what you want those chocolate tarts for, you sex addict!"

"Come on. It'll be fun. I know how much you crave chocolate during that time, so I'm helping you out. Is that so wrong?" I gripped her hips. "Think of how sexy it'll be," I whispered in her ear.

"Hey, everyone!" Sam shouted. "Dad just called. Celeste is in labor."

"She's not due for another seven weeks," I said.

"I know. We all need to get to the hospital. He doesn't sound good."

"Shit. Let's go." I grabbed Grace's hand.

CHAPTER 46

Simon

We all drove to the hospital and Sam sent our dad a text message to let him know we were waiting in the labor and delivery waiting room. Julia went home because she was exhausted and couldn't stand anymore, and Alex had to take the kids home. So, it was myself, Grace, my brothers, and Emilia.

"Thanks for coming boys." My father walked over and hugged us.

"Of course, Dad. How is Celeste?"

"They're prepping her now for a c-section. I'm scared boys. Really scared."

"Henry." Emilia walked over and placed her hand on his back. "A baby born this early, especially a girl, has the best chances. She's going to be fine. Celeste has done everything right and she's healthy."

"Thank you, Emilia. Celeste is asking for you. She would like you to be in there as well when the baby is born so you can tend to Nora right away."

"Of course. I have privileges here. I'll go get changed."

She walked over and gave Sebastian a kiss. "I'll see you later. I love you."

"I love you too, baby. Please don't let anything happen to my sister."

"I won't."

"Both Nora and Celeste are going to be fine, Dad." I hooked my arm around him.

"Yeah, Dad, and we'll all be right here when she's born," Sam spoke.

"We're here for all of you, Dad." Stefan hugged him.

"Thank you, my sons. I better get in there. I'll keep you updated."

I let out a sigh as I ran my hand through my hair.

"They're going to be okay," Grace said as she wrapped her arms around my waist.

"I sure hope so. If anything happens to either one of them, I don't know what my father will do."

"We have to keep calm and think only positive thoughts."

"Sam and I are going to grab some coffees. Do you guys want one?" Stefan asked as he walked over.

"Sure," I said.

"Yeah, bro," Sebastian spoke.

"I'll go with them." Grace gave my hand a gentle squeeze.

Sebastian and I walked over and sat down by the window.

"Bro, this reminds me of when we were waiting to hear about you after you got shot."

"Did you think I was going to be okay?"

"Honestly, we weren't sure." He glanced over at me. "We just weren't sure."

"And look. I'm perfectly fine, and Nora and Celeste will be too."

A few moments later, Sam, Stefan, and Grace walked back in with our coffees.

"Thanks, babe." I took the cup from Grace's hand.

"Did Simon ever tell you guys about how he was being held at gunpoint the night we went after Ives?"

"No. What the hell, bro?" Stefan said.

"Why wouldn't you tell us something like that?" Sam asked.

"Oh, that's right. That was the night she almost killed me."

"I did not almost kill you." She rolled her eyes.

"Yes. Yes, you did."

"What happened?" Sebastian chuckled.

"So, this asshole grabs me and points his gun to my head and tells Grace to drop her gun. And guess what? She wouldn't. The two of them go back and forth. She's calling him a cockroach and he tells her he's going to kill me. Do you know what she said?"

"What did she say?" Sam asked.

"She said 'do what you have to do.'"

"Oh shit!" Stefan clapped as he let out a laugh.

"Obviously, he didn't kill you." Sebastian smirked.

"No. Because while he was holding a gun to my head, she shot him in the forehead, missing me by millimeters."

"Oh my God. He's being very dramatic," Grace said.

"No, I'm not. If she would have been off by a fraction, that bullet would have hit me."

All three of my brothers started laughing.

"I can't believe you didn't tell us that." Sebastian laughed.

Before I could say anything, our father walked in, and the room went silent as we stared at him.

"Dad?" I spoke.

"Celeste and the baby are doing just fine."

We all let out a sigh of relief.

"Nora is three pounds two ounces, and she's absolutely beautiful."

"Isn't that about what we each weighed?" I asked.

"Yes, son. She has to spend some time in the NICU, but

SANDI LYNN

Emilia and the other doctors said she is strong and she's going to be okay. She's a little fighter, that one. She's like her brothers." He smiled.

"Aw, Dad." We all got up from our seats and gave him a hug.

"We're really happy to hear that," Sam said.

"When will we be able to see our sister?" Stefan asked.

"I talked to the nurse and told her little Nora has four brothers that she needs to meet. You'll be able to see her through the glass tomorrow. Thank you, boys, for being here. I really appreciate it."

"There's nowhere else we'd be, Dad."

"You boys go home and get some rest. There's no need for you to stick around. I'll call you and let you know how things are going."

"Give Celeste our best, Dad, and tell her we'll come by tomorrow to see her," Sam said.

~

One Week Later

"I have a surprise for you," I traced the outline of her lips as we lay in bed and stared at each other.

"What kind of surprise?" she asked with a beautiful smile.

"You'll see." The corners of my mouth curved upward as I kissed her lips, climbed out of bed, and pulled on a pair of pants.

Grace grabbed her silk robe, slipped it on, and followed me downstairs. Opening the door that led to the garage, I grabbed her hand.

"What do you think?" I pointed to the surfboard that sat up against the wall with a large red bow around it.

238

She looked at me with a grin across her face. "Is that for me?"

"It is. I had it custom made. It was delivered to Stefan's house yesterday, so I had him put it in the garage while we were at work last night."

"Simon, I love it so much. Thank you." She wrapped her arms around me and kissed my lips.

"You're welcome. I wanted you to have one of your own, so you don't have to borrow Emilia's anymore. Since it's our day off, how about we go test it out?"

"I'd love to."

We went back inside and put on our wetsuits, grabbed our boards, and ran down to the beach. Putting our boards in the water, we paddled out and straddled our boards side by side each other.

"How does it feel?" I asked.

"It feels amazing." She smiled. "Thank you again. I love you so much."

"I love you too." I leaned in and our lips met.

"The water is for surfing not making out!" I heard Sebastian shout from the beach.

Turning around, I flipped him off and he laughed.

Later that evening, we met my family at Four Kinds for dinner after we stopped by the hospital and visited Nora. She was doing well, and the doctor told my father that she would most likely be ready to come home in a couple of weeks.

"How did Grace like her surfboard?" Stefan asked as he walked over.

"She loved it." I stared at Grace from across the room as she stood talking to Julia and Alex.

Stefan placed his hand on my shoulder. "I'm really happy for the two of you, bro."

"Thanks, brother." I gave him a smile.

I stood there and stared at every member of my family.

Sam and Julia, Stefan, Alex and the kids, Sebastian and Emilia, and my beautiful girlfriend Grace. Soon, this room would be filled with three more babies, and I couldn't ask for a more perfect life or family.

"What are you doing?" Grace walked over and hooked her arm around me.

"Just looking at my perfect family." I smiled. "I would do anything to protect them."

"I know you would, and so would I."

"Have I told you how much I love you, Detective Grace Adams?"

"Even when I put your life in danger?" A smirk crossed her lips.

"Even when you put my life in danger." Our mouths met for a kiss. "By the way, we never did discuss what happened the other day when we were going after those two suspects. Remember I said we were going to talk about it when we got home?"

She kissed my cheek and started to walk away.

"You really need to stop being so dramatic." She turned and gave me a wink, and I let out a chuckle.

"Hey, bro. Can you run over to the bar and grab a bottle of Pinot?" Sebastian asked.

"Yeah. I need to hit the bathroom first."

After washing my hands, I headed towards the bar and furrowed my brows when I saw a familiar face sitting there.

"Shaun?" I stepped behind the bar.

"Simon?" He smiled. "What the hell? It's good to see you again."

"You too. What are you doing here?"

"I was looking up top restaurants and this one came up. I figured I'd give it a try. I'm just waiting for my table to become available."

"I didn't realize you were still in California."

240

"Yeah. My business here ran longer than I thought. May I ask why you're behind the bar?" His brow arched.

"This is my brother's restaurant."

"No shit?" He smiled. "How many brothers do you have?"

"Three. We're quadruplets."

"Quadruplets? Damn. And one of your brothers owns this place?"

"Yeah. He also owns another restaurant in downtown L.A. called Emilia's. In fact, here come my brothers now."

I held my hand up and gestured for them to come over to the bar.

"Where's that bottle of Pinot?" Sebastian asked as he walked over with Sam and Stefan.

"Shaun, I'd like you to meet my brothers. This is Sebastian. He owns this place."

"Nice to meet you, man." Shaun extended his hand.

"And this is Sam."

"Nice to meet you, Shaun." Sam shook his hand.

"And this is Stefan."

"Nice to meet you." He shook Stefan's hand.

~

*S*haun

I stood there and stared at the four men who were my brothers. Brothers I didn't even know I had until three months ago. They had no idea who I was, but when the time was right, they would. My plan was already in motion to get to know my family. The family who shared the same blood as mine. Let the family drama begin.

Thank you for reading Four of a Kind! I hope you enjoyed it!

*W*hat's in store for the Kind brothers now that they've met the handsome stranger who just rolled into town? Find out in the next installment of the Kind Brothers Series, Five of a Kind.

PREORDER HERE

I'd love for you to join my romance tribe by following me on social media and subscribing to my newsletter to keep up with my new releases, sales, cover reveals, and more!

Newsletter
Website
Facebook
Instagram
Bookbub
Goodreads

Looking for more romance reads about billionaires, second chances and sports? Check out my other romance novels and escape to another world and from the daily grind of life – one book at a time.

Series:

Forever Series
Forever Black (Forever, Book 1)
Forever You (Forever, Book 2)
Forever Us (Forever, Book 3)
Being Julia (Forever, Book 4)
Collin (Forever, Book 5)
A Forever Family (Forever, Book 6)
A Forever Christmas (Holiday short story)

Wyatt Brothers
Love, Lust & A Millionaire (Wyatt Brothers, Book 1)
Love, Lust & Liam (Wyatt Brothers, Book 2)

A Millionaire's Love
Lie Next to Me (A Millionaire's Love, Book 1)
When I Lie with You (A Millionaire's Love, Book 2)

Happened Series
Then You Happened (Happened Series, Book 1)
Then We Happened (Happened Series, Book 2)

Redemption Series
Carter Grayson (Redemption Series, Book 1)
Chase Calloway (Redemption Series, Book 2)
Jamieson Finn (Redemption Series, Book 3)
Damien Prescott (Redemption Series, Book 4)

Interview Series
The Interview: New York & Los Angeles Part 1
The Interview: New York & Los Angeles Part 2

Love Series:
Love In Between (Love Series, Book 1)
The Upside of Love (Love Series, Book 2)

Wolfe Brothers
Elijah Wolfe (Wolfe Brothers, Book 1)
Nathan Wolfe (Wolfe Brothers, Book 2)
Mason Wolfe (Wolfe Brothers, Book 3)

Kind Brothers
One of a Kind
Two of a Kind
Three of a Kind
Four of a Kind
Five of a Kind

Standalone Books:

The Billionaire's Christmas Baby
His Proposed Deal
The Secret He Holds
The Seduction of Alex Parker

Something About Lorelei
One Night in London
The Exception
Corporate Assets
A Beautiful Sight
The Negotiation
Defense
The Con Artist
#Delete
Behind His Lies
One Night in Paris
Perfectly You
The Escort
The Ring
The Donor
Rewind
Remembering You
When I'm With You
LOGAN (A Hockey Romance)
The Merger
Baby Drama
Unspoken
The Property Brokers

Made in the USA
Coppell, TX
16 February 2022

73677559R00144